PEAR SEASON

Also by Sally Small

DARK CHOCOLATE

TWO SLOUGHS

PEAR SEASON

stories

For Gretchen, who taught my children to love books

With love,

Sally Small

SALLY SMALL

iUniverse, Inc.
Bloomington

PEAR SEASON

iUniverse books may be ordered through booksellers or by contacting:

iUniverse
1663 Liberty Drive
Bloomington, IN 47403
www.iuniverse.com
1-800-Authors (1-800-288-4677)

ISBN: 978-1-4759-9443-8 (sc)
ISBN: 978-1-4759-9444-5 (ebk)

Printed in the United States of America

iUniverse rev. date: 06/11/2013

CONTENTS

Two of the stories in this collection, ELEVEN and DEER CAMP, were published previously, in slightly different form, in DARK CHOCOLATE by San Francisco State University.

Thank you: Sandy Bails, George Hartzell, Shirley Hobart, Jeff Kunkel, John Lyons, Rob Moser, John Small, Mary Small and, of course, Sandy Small

For my mother and father

THE FOURTH OF JULY PARADE

My brother and I couldn't figure it out. Why would our cousin Harold want to come stay with us for the Fourth of July? Harold had told us about the Fourth of July rodeo in Modesto, where they sold cotton candy and gave away $100 cash prizes, about the fireworks in the Modesto Civic Park near Harold's house—just like World War II, Harold said, bombs exploding all over the sky and a grand American flag outlined in pinwheels at the end. Harold owned a complete set of the Green Hornet comic books for the last three years. He went downtown alone to the movies every Saturday. We were awed by his urbanity, impressed by his age. He was six months older than my brother Jimmy, two years older than I.

Harold didn't overwhelm our mother, however. She may have seen in his yellow dandelion hair and his red ears a replica of her own brother, Harold's father. She adored them both. Either one of them could collapse her into a chair gasping with laughter. But she had a big-sister way of saying, "I'll settle his hash. Where is he?" that was instantly effective. We appealed to our mother for inspiration, something to dazzle our cousin Harold.

Mother straightened up. Mother was usually bent over something, the vacuum, an open oven door, a pile of laundry. "Nonsense," she said. "He'll have the time of his life. Go pick up your room or he won't be able to squeeze in there to go to bed."

"But Ma," we whined. "Come on, Ma."

"And throw away that dead lizard while you're at it, Jimmy."

We fled out the back door, letting the screen slam, and climbed on our bikes for a tour of inspection. Yesterday the town of Pear Blossom had suited us fine—not much town and plenty of gaps and cracks where the fields poked through: ditches that hadn't been cemented over, trees that hid tree houses, fences with holes in them. Today as we pedaled into town, arms folded in unspoken challenge (I can ride farther with no hands that you can), we looked at the town through Harold's eyes.

There were four straight streets one block long, named First Street, Second Street, Third Street and Fourth Street, plus a street at each end to square things up. We rode disconsolately down every one. The Catholic Church was built at one end; the Presbyterian Church at the other. The Big Store, Ike's Café and the gas station were on the other side of the river.

"There's nothing to do here," moaned Jimmy, leaning to the inside as he negotiated the corner on Fourth Street.

I was pedaling fast to catch up. "What's he coming for anyway? Why doesn't he stay in Modesto?"

The houses were wood, white and square, raised half a floor off the ground with no basements because of the wet winters. Most of the houses had little triangle roofs over the doors, mounded with honeysuckle or morning glory. There was a square patch of Bermuda grass out in front of each house, with a smaller rectangle of lawn between the sidewalk and the street. This was to provide "chores" for the children of Pear Blossom. The grass had to be mowed once a week.

If you knew who lived in them, the houses took on character. Mr. Steiner on Second Street shot cats. Three doors down, the Hammonds gave out homemade fudge at Halloween. Further along the block, Mrs. Spencer grew championship camellias at the side of her house, camellias with names as long as race horses. She had won ribbons at the Camellia Festival in Sacramento. But Harold wouldn't know all this. All Harold would see were dull old houses, as though some farmer had decided, instead of the usual tomatoes or corn or sugar beets, to plant square white houses this year.

We were doubly uneasy that Harold had chosen the Fourth of July to visit. The Fourth of July Parade was the biggest event of the year in Pear Blossom, and we had told Harold all about it, embroidering a little here and there to compensate for the rodeo in Modesto. We suspected Harold might be expecting too much.

The Fourth of July coincided with pear season in Pear Blossom, a hectic time, so by informal agreement no preparations for the parade began more than a day or two in advance. The decorations were elaborate—homemade floats, decorated tricycles, dogs pulling wagons and family drill teams, but it was last-minute feverish activity, and the drug store always ran out of red or blue crepe paper.

This year ten members of Miss Harvie's grammar school band were playing in the parade for the first time. We had never had actual music in the parade before. We had always marched to the brrring of tricycle bells, with an occasional fire siren thrown in for festivity. The impetus of a real band mobilized the whole town. The planning became more involved, which added another worry for my brother and me.

Our mother was "artistic." She insisted we build a float because Dad had a pear trailer to put it on. A pear trailer is a flatbed trailer six feet by twelve feet long, built very close to the ground and towed by whatever piece of equipment is available. In the orchard the trailer held the bins the pickers filled with pears. To our mother it was a stage. She invented grandiose themes, for which she dyed yards of old sheets. It was then our father's responsibility to engineer the whole affair so that it wouldn't fall down when pulled around on a pear trailer. The costumes our mother designed were ingenious and complicated. She didn't sew much, but she could staple and glue with a flair. We would be torn between embarrassment over what she made us wear and the possibility of winning first place.

Cousin Harold arrived on the third of July. He came on the bus by himself with his suitcase, a buck knife in a scabbard on his belt, and a paper bag full of Double Bubble bubble-gum. Mother sent him in to change into his bathing suit and then put him right to work out in the front yard with the rest of us painting the cardboard boat that was to dominate our float. We were portraying Washington crossing the Delaware, and the boat Mother had concocted was an elaborate compromise between the Mayflower and a refrigerator

3

packing crate. She had insisted on masts and sails although our father had dug up pictures to support his view that Washington crossed the Delaware in little more than a rowboat.

"Don't be ridiculous," Mother retorted. "The float needs height."

Harold was an enthusiastic painter, and he seemed to like the idea of painting in a bathing suit so he could make all the mess he wanted. One side looked pretty good by the time we were through. We had to water the poster paint quite a bit to finish the back side, but Mother said it looked as if the fog had come in. It would be fine.

Our parade always began at ten o'clock the morning of the Fourth in front of the Fire House next to the Presbyterian Church. Nobody tacked posters to telephone poles, no committee strung up banners over the street. Everybody just knew the parade started in front of the Fire House at ten o'clock.

The Fourth of July is always hot in Pear Blossom, and by nine o'clock in the morning we kids were roasting in our costumes. Harold, Jimmy and I, plus our little brother Robbie and the two Bryan boys from next door, were uniformed in long-sleeved, red sweatshirts with roughly parallel rows of double breasted tin foil buttons stapled down the front. Our chests were criss-crossed by white sheeting straps cut with pinking shears. Over this outfit the officers (Harold, Jimmy and I) sported old navy blue jackets of our fathers and our neighbors' fathers with lots of gold Christmas tinsel tacked on the shoulders. Our pants were tucked into irrigating boots. On our heads we wore white mops, tied neatly at the nape of the neck with red ribbon, and navy tri-corner hats. The thermometer had already climbed to ninety-three degrees.

In these costumes we were frantically attaching the last blue waves of butcher paper around the edge of the cardboard boat, sweating and arguing over who was doing the most work. By 9:30 Harold and Jimmy flatly refused to ride on the float.

"You get right up there!" My mother pointed menacingly with her stapler. "You're George Washington," she roared at my brother. You have the spy glass."

"It's a paper towel roll," my brother griped.

And my father had to threaten both boys quite a bit before he hit on a sufficiently awful alternative to riding on the float.

When we finally lurched into line in front of the Fire House and saw the McCarthy's float, we realized it could have been worse. Mrs. McCarthy had come up with a Men from Mars theme. The McCarthy girls slouched around a silver foil spaceship wearing long underwear dyed bright green, bobbing their paper mache heads, which were about eighteen inches in diameter with pipe-cleaner antennas and no air holes.

The Hammond family pulled in behind the Men from Mars. Debbie Hammond was decked out as the Statue of Liberty in a white sheet with a torch of oleander branches in one hand and a tablet (which was actually a Betty Crocker cookbook) in the other. She was struggling to keep her balance on top of an upside down pear bin that slid back and forth across their pear trailer while her little brothers, costumed as the huddled masses, strove to steady her.

The fire sirens sounded at ten o'clock, right on schedule. The town dogs howled, and the town's two fire trucks, all spit-and-polished for the occasion by the volunteer fire department, set off down Second Street at five miles per hour, lights flashing, sirens blaring. The fire trucks always led the parade carrying any leftover kids. Behind the fire trucks came Miss Harvie's grammar school band, playing The Stars and Stripes Forever. Since the band had never mastered marching and looking at their music simultaneously, they sat on folding chairs on a pear trailer pulled by Jeff Berry with his new Chalmers tractor. Miss Harvie clutched at the back of Jeff Berry's tractor with one hand and beat time with the other.

Behind the band came the tricycles and bicycles with red, white and blue crepe paper wound through the spokes and little American flags on the handlebars. There were one or two dogs, washed and decorated with ribbons, although dog entries tended to get into fights with spectator dogs and were not encouraged.

The floats came next, about five or six in all. The Men from Mars, Tom Sawyer. The Mendelsons usually chose an exotic theme because they had big clumps of pampas grass growing on their ranch. This year's theme appeared to have something to do with Cleopatra. It was hard to tell because their signs had smeared.

Following the floats in a skittish procession came the horses, four or five horses ridden by the local twelve-year-old girls. The same horses had been ridden in the parade for years, sold by older generations of girls to younger girls, so everyone knew which horses to look out for.

The parade customarily went three times counter clockwise around the middle block, down Second Street, around the corner, back up Third Street, across in front of the Fire House and around again. Anybody who didn't live on the middle block stood in front of the Fire House to watch. The band rested until they got close to the Fire House and then struck up their single tune.

The first time around the block the masts of George Washington's ship caught a tree in front of the Barton's house, and our sails came down enveloping George Washington and his troops. The parade had to stop for a minute in the middle of the block while Dad furled our sails and left them on the Barton's lawn.

The second time around, an antique car club from Sacramento pulled into line, having heard about the parade, apparently, but misjudging its tenor. They looked ridiculous—grownups in authentic period costumes in the Pear Blossom parade. Their plunkety engines spooked the horses. Not only that, they made the parade too long. The fire trucks at the front of the parade began to catch up with the antique cars at the back.

The third time past the Fire House, Billy Barnes threw a firecracker right under Caroline Cramer's horse, Honey, a great tub of a mare with a perverse impatience for pageantry. Honey went off like a rotund Roman candle, past the floats, through the bicycles, up onto the sidewalk, straight down the little squares of front lawn, churning up clumps of grass like a rototiller. Caroline's cowboy hat flew off, and she screamed and cried and clung to the saddle horn with both hands, letting the reins fly.

Several fathers dropped their movie cameras and joined the chase after Honey and Caroline, and some of the boys on decorated bikes took off, too. All the dogs on the street began to bark. Honey tried to jump Mrs. Spencer's camellia bushes about half-way down the block but missed, and Mrs. Spencer grabbed a garden rake and ran after the horse with murder in her eye. Then Honey rounded the corner onto Third Street and caught up with the antique cars at the rear of the parade, followed by the dogs and the bikes and the fathers, terrifying the drivers in the cars and causing a Model T to bump into the Packard in front of it.

Honey headed straight for the barn and didn't stop until she got there. Miss Harvie's band kept right on playing The Stars and Stripes Forever, though the rhythm was somewhat syncopated now. Debbie held her oleander torch aloft, and afterwards the volunteer firemen gave out rainbow popsicles to everybody except the antique car club, who left early.

Debbie Hammond's Statue of Liberty won first place, with special mention to Washington Crossing the Delaware. There were no prizes—just the honor of the thing. Jimmy said it wasn't fair because it's easy to dress up like huddled masses. Mrs. Spencer said later that she guessed it was almost time to prune her camellias anyway, and we all agreed it had been the best Fourth of July Parade ever.

Harold wants to come next year.

HORSE STORY

It was an adult remark, casual, possibly insincere. Like "Help yourself" when they meant you could take two. But Jenny was a child, almost ten years old. She burrowed into her uncle's words, clinging like a flea.

"If it's born on your birthday, Jenny, the foal is yours." Her uncle had said it. Her mother's cautioning and her father's rough dismissal of the remark couldn't budge her.

"Don't take your Uncle Buck too seriously, Jenny," her mother said.

"That was just talk," her father said.

Still, her uncle had said it. He might not mean it, but he might. What if he meant it?

It had happened like this. Her Uncle Buck lived next door in a gaunt white house just like theirs. Both houses had sagging porches across the front and screened porches in back off the kitchen. Both houses could use some paint. Uncle Buck was her father's younger brother, a bachelor. He managed the open land. Her father managed the orchards. Her father was serious, level-headed. Uncle Buck was funny. As a young man he had been "wild," according to Jenny's mother. He had team-roped on the rodeo circuit before his accident. Now he walked with a kind of a tilt. His left leg was a full inch shorter than his right so that he listed to the left. But he swung his arms at such a jaunty angle that it seemed to Jenny he was always about to pirouette. Neighbors were always respectful of her father, but they laughed with pleasure when Uncle Buck waltzed into the room, his deep, booming voice full of fun.

Uncle Buck was still a horseman. He kept horses in the pasture back of their houses, actually a series of horses traded with old Mr. Simpson, the river horse trader, in elaborate negotiations that included saddles and two head of cattle or an outboard motor with no starter rope. Maybe a disc plow thrown in to seal the deal. Her uncle used to say he lost a little on every trade, but the education was worth it.

This particular time Mr. Simpson had accidentally sold her uncle a mare in foal. Simpson was irritated about the slip-up and tried to get her uncle to give back the chain saw that had been part of the bargain. This pleased her uncle, and it was while he was leaning against her front porch, his collar turned up against the freezing February wind, his duck hunting cap pulled down, chuckling to her dad about the deal, that she had asked him about the foal.

"What are you going to do with the foal?" She stared at her uncle over a dark red apple, shuddering from the cold and the seriousness of the thought.

"I'll tell you what, Peanut. If it's born on your birthday, the foal is yours." Then he remembered something about the planting, and the two men had gone on to talk about hybrid seed without even a backward thought of that foal.

Jenny sat down on the porch swing. The green and white striped canvas cushions had been taken in for the winter. She rocked unsteadily on the springs. She was tall for her age and skinny, with hair too straight and legs too long and feet too big. She wore thick glasses to correct a wandering eye, but even so she squinted and tripped a lot. Her left knee was permanently skinned. She sat picking at the scab on her knee. She was stunned.

From then on, every day after school Jenny slogged out through the mud to the pasture behind the house. She watched the new mare belly out, brushed her thick winter coat, stroked her dark bay flanks when she wasn't fidgety, brought her carrot tops and pieces of apple and celery sticks from her lunch box, begged her to keep that foal inside until March 22. The mare wasn't used to the girl and seemed irritated by the attention. She nipped when she took lettuce and carrot tops from Jenny's hand and turned her back when the girl tried to curry her or comb her dark mane, lowering her ears, glowering over her shoulder. Still Jenny persisted week after week, badgering the mare, whispering softly to her, bribing her, blowing gently on her muzzle.

Jenny became tongue-tied in her uncle's presence. Her Uncle Buck had been her pal. He had danced her around the kitchen. He had taught her how to ride a horse. She hated the women who came to visit him. She had always imagined he would wait until she grew up and then marry her. Now she was shy and silent when he dropped by.

February dragged on, damp and cold, shrouded in tule fog. Along the Sacramento River day and night melted into different shades of gray. Stubborn rain beat the pasture into a muddy mire. The mare churned up the mud in her restless pacing until it matted her woolly coat and sucked at Jenny's black irrigating boots. The river rose. The high water oozed through the old levee in front of their house. The drainage ditches filled and the fields in the middle of their island flooded. Flocks of geese floated in the fog. The mare stood on a high spot under the apple tree fetlock-deep in mud, her head lowered, her flanks to the wind. What if the foal dropped early, spewed into the muck of the pasture? Every morning Jenny knelt on her bed and looked out her upstairs window through the bare branches of the old apple tree into the pasture. Still no foal.

Meanwhile Uncle Buck developed disturbing tendencies. Her mother and father got into a fight one night because of him. Uncle Buck had promised to take Granny to the doctor, and he hadn't shown up.

"You just can't ever depend on him," her mother fumed.

Her father sighed. "He means to. He just forgets sometimes."

"Well, he's undependable. It's ridiculous," said her mother.

Ordinarily Jenny would have waded in and taken Uncle Buck's side. Now she worried.

Then Uncle Buck came up with a girlfriend in Stockton. Charlene. It seemed like he was never around, and when he was, all he talked about was Charlene. He got his hair styled and started growing a mustache.

"What?" huffed her mother. "Is he trying to look like a grownup?"

Jenny didn't see him for days at a time, and when she did he was always rushing off to Stockton. Jenny came to see Uncle Buck in a whole new light. She remembered instances in the past when he had promised to take her riding and then "forgotten." She could remember spending whole afternoons on the porch watching for his pickup.

Her mother warned her that it might have been just "a figure of speech." "He might not mean that he actually intended to give you the foal," she said. From her mother's tone of voice she surmised that Uncle Buck wasn't quite a grownup, someone who could be relied upon. He was more like a playmate, like Annie McCarthy, who had claimed to be Jenny's best friend and then invited Janet Sarah to go to the circus.

Jenny continued to visit the mare every day. While she fed her apples and carrots and oats she stole from the cereal box in the kitchen she confided in the mare, and the mare listened solemnly. She had grown used to Jenny. When Jenny blew softly in the mare's muzzle and scratched behind her ears, sometimes the mare would lean against her, urging her to scratch some more. Jenny told the mare about her fears, how unpredictable Uncle Buck could be, how he'd never even mentioned the subject again. Not once.

March came. The air warmed first, stirred by the yellow-breasted meadowlark who sang his burbling song from the pasture fence posts. The soggy ground began to waken, a tender green tremor across the fields. When the north wind blew, it seemed to Jenny that the whole island would burst open like the pale pink apple blossoms fringed in young leaves or the green duck's eggs nestled in the cattails along the ditch. When Jenny ran through the wind out to the pasture, the wind seemed to catch and tangle inside her until she felt she too might burst. Even the mare caught the excitement in the wind, tossing her head, whinnying as she plodded across the pasture for the treat Jenny held out to her. The mare's belly, heavy with promise, swayed beneath her.

Three days before her birthday Jenny woke and looked out of her upstairs window. The mare wasn't under the apple tree. The mare was always under the apple tree! She reached for her glasses and scanned the part of the pasture she could see from the window, then tugged on her rubber irrigating boots, grabbed her jacket and bounded down the stairs. She raced through the kitchen, hardly noticing her parents and her Uncle Buck, who were sitting around the kitchen table drinking coffee. She let the screen door slam, stumbled on the back steps. She raced for the pasture fence, her flannel nightgown flapping under her jacket.

In the far corner of the pasture the mare stood, and beside her on the damp ground in a jumble of legs lay the foal, straggly brown with a pale pink muzzle. The foal raised his head and straightened his front legs as she crept closer. Then he collapsed, surprised by her and the pasture and his own unfamiliar limbs. Jenny knelt in the dew-drenched weeds along the fence shivering and staring at the foal, and the foal stared back, blinking his long eyelashes. They had their own shy, silent conversation in the quiet morning.

"You couldn't wait, could you," she said silently to the foal. "You were in too much of a hurry to be born. You couldn't wait for my birthday." She pulled her jacket tight around her chest.

The sun angled up over the house and touched the foal and the girl. Jenny watched the colt's hair begin to dry and fluff like a dandelion. She didn't notice her Uncle Buck walking up behind her.

"Fine looking little feller, don't you think?"

Jenny looked up at Uncle Buck. "What are you going to do with him?"

"Oh, his ma won't let me do a thing with him for a couple of months. Then I don't know."

Uncle Buck had forgotten all about his promise to her. He hadn't been serious. Her father had been right. It had been just talk.

"I could probably get a good price for him." Uncle Buck leaned against a fence post.

"Sell him?"

"Why not?" Uncle Buck chuckled, "Old man Simpson would be mad as a wet hen."

Jenny took one last look at the foal lying in the sun, drowsy and warm, then she stumbled back to the house.

She ran up the stairs in her muddy irrigating boots and flung herself on her bed.

Her mother sighed, wiped her hands on her apron and followed Jenny up the stairs. She sat beside her daughter on the bed and rubbed her back. "Your dad and I tried to warn you, Jenny."

Jenny's head remained pressed to her pillow.

"It's probably just as well. Taking care of a colt is a big job."

Jenny's back heaved with sobs.

But Jenny couldn't stay away from the foal. After school that day she stood at the pasture fence with a bunch of carrots and a handful of Quaker Oats. She moved slowly, quietly crooning to the mare, and by the next day she was able to get inside the pasture, not close, but inside the fence.

Two days later, Saturday, her birthday, she woke early and took a whole apple out to the mare. As the mare stood munching the apple out of Jenny's hand, Jenny felt a little nudge at her elbow. The curious foal had come up beside her and nuzzled her arm. Jenny froze, watching the mare's ears, but the mare seemed content to chew on her apple. Jenny touched the velvet muzzle of the colt. His whiskers twitched, but he didn't back away. He nibbled at her shirt. She giggled.

"No tickling," she whispered. "Thank you, she said to the colt silently. "That's the best birthday present ever."

"He seems to like you."

Jenny hadn't heard her uncle come into the pasture. He scratched his mare behind the ears, and she snuffled with pleasure.

"He's fine," Jenny said softly.

"You still want him?"

"You mean the foal?" Jenny asked warily.

"You invested more love in him before he was born than most creatures get in a lifetime."

Through her thick glasses she searched his eyes for signs of teasing.

"I told you he was yours if he came for your birthday, Peanut. I never break promises to true believers. You'll have to share him with his ma for a while. She'll see to that. Now go get some clothes on before your ma has apoplexy."

Jenny had stopped listening. She was staring at the colt warming in the sunshine. The world of mud puddles and dirt clods, the confusing, contradictory world of adults shone all around her on that still, spring morning. She inched closer to the colt, watching the mare's ears. If she was patient, she might be able to pat his neck before the day was over.

ELEVEN

The sun was up by now. A heavy sun sunk low along the sky. It turned the corn stubble brassy, burnished the cattails and the ditch willows, drew steam out of the dirt clods along the road. Pheasant season, when the corn was off and sold, and whatever could go wrong had already gone wrong, and getting up at five in the morning wouldn't help it. The last long sun before the tule fogs and rains washed the valley dishwater gray, and winter set in for good.

A rusted pickup jolted along the dirt road. Dan drove, both hands on the wheel, elbows out, legs spread, as if he were accustomed to sitting a horse with a bum gait. His eyes were on the ditch. The boy took up very little room beside him on the bench seat of the pickup. He sat close to his door, twiddling the knob of the window crank. Eleven. He was eleven. Seemed like no matter what, he couldn't get older.

"Don't do that, Son. You'll twist it off."

Jimmy stopped. His sideways glance caught the sharp edge of his father's face. The boy's chin sank into his jacket collar, and he leaned back against the seat.

Dan wished he hadn't had to start out that way. But the pickup was falling apart quick enough by itself. He pulled up at the far end of the cornfield. "Well, you gonna get out? Or just sit here waiting for the pheasant to come to you." He had meant that to be a joke.

The boy looked at him with dull confused eyes.

"Now, Honey," Dan said, "you've been giving those tin cans hell back behind the shed. Let's see how you do when these old daddy pheasants come exploding out of the stubble, all whirr and feathers." Dan let the dog out of the back of the pickup and sat with the boy on the tailgate, trying to sort out his son's sullenness. "You understand why we only shoot cocks?" He put his arm around the boy. "Every hen out there means four, maybe six chicks next spring. You understand?"

"Yeah."

"Well then, tie your bootlace and come on."

Dan handed the boy his .410 shotgun. "Now you be careful, hear? Stay even with me and don't swing around. These old devils can scare the daylights out of you."

The dog, a broad-chested Irish setter, danced around his master whining, drooling.

The boy slouched silently against the side of the pickup looking down at his gun, his finger tracing the fine lines along the side of the barrel.

Dan was irritated by the boy's lack of enthusiasm. "Watch it," he snapped. "You'll get mud up the barrel. Don't ever let your gun drag like that." He stalked off.

Jimmy trudged after him, trying to keep up, squinting as if the whole world blinded him, as if he looked at it through the glint of his gun barrel. He squinted, rubbed his nose, fumbled the shells in his jacket pocket. The corn stubble came up nearly to his knees; thick stalks hacked sharp by the harvester. He watched his father stride along and the dog race back and forth across the field, nose stretched out, tail streaming.

The dog stopped, forged as one piece upon the golden field, front leg cocked, nose down, tail rigid.

"Now, easy, Honey. I'll kick it up. Ready? Don't shoot till I say."

A roar of wings shook the earth beneath the boy's feet, rent the stubble, shattered the sky. The boy staggered, tripped, raised his gun, shot.

"No," Dan shouted. "No. Hen!"

The dog raced out at the sound of the shot, but the hen rose and flew straight up the field, dipping down behind the check. Dan whistled the dog back. Jimmy broke his gun and picked the empty shell out of the barrel, all thumbs. He put the empty shell in his other pocket, took a new shell, placed it in the chamber, fingers shaking, snapped the gun shut, slid the safety up. He didn't look at the dog or at his father.

Dan watched him, helpless, wondering if the boy was going to throw up. They walked on side by side while Dan thought of things he might say. The field was still again, except for the dog working out ahead of them.

"OK, this time take a bead on him, but wait for me to call it."

Again the dog quivered like an arrow shot into a straw target. Dan kicked the bird out, jumped back. "Shoot," he shouted. "Shoot."

Again the dog leaped out at the sound of the shot. The man whistled him back. "That wasn't bad," Dan said. "You shot behind him, was all."

Jimmy rubbed his shoulder, then tugged at his jacket. His father pretended not to notice, pretended everything was fine, even the weather, though they needed rain. Nothing you can do about the weather, so why talk about it.

They were nearly at the other end of the field. The boy had shot at four cocks. Clean misses.

Every afternoon since school started, Jimmy had practiced with the cans. He set them against the shed. Sometimes his father would stop to throw a couple into the air for him. He had cleaned his shotgun a dozen times since September, till his room smelled of Hoppe's #9 solvent from the rags he kept stuffed in a coffee can beside his bed. "If you're not ready now, you never will be," his father had said.

"Move up," Dan said. "They'll start coming out fast now. They've been sneaking along ahead of us. They'll make a break for it now."

Two hens whirled off to the right and down behind the cattails. A cock sprang straight into the sun, blinding the boy in his gun's glare. The dog rushed in on another cock before the boy could reload his single barrel. He wrestled with his gun while the sound of the birds exploded in his head.

The dog stared at him, disgusted, then brushed right by him, ignored him. Jimmy kicked the dog savagely. The dog yelped and fell away.

17

"Stop that!" Dan roared. "Stop it." He snatched the boy by the collar. "Don't ever let me catch you kicking my dog again. Hear me? Any dog. What's the matter with you?"

The dog circled, slunk around behind the man. The man rolled a dirt clod over with his boot, eyed the boy, put his free arm around him. Jimmy turned away.

"It's not easy, Honey. Nobody said it was easy." Dan's voice was cracked and rusty. "It takes time. You got to work at it."

Jimmy raised his chin, shot his father a look of pure hate, right between the eyes, then pulled his chin back down, clenched his jaw, locked up his face.

Dan saw the look, kept silent, broke off a stalk along the ditch, examined it although he knew it was only curly dock, no-good weed.

He turned back down the field. "Now we'll walk this side," he said. "The smart ones are all still in here. We only scared the hens and the silly youngsters." The word "youngsters" stuck in his throat, but he'd said it, so he let it go. "Now, don't let your gun stop on you. Nice easy swing, like when I throw the cans." The boy was walking slack, dragging his feet through the stubble. "And be ready," Dan said irritably.

Again the dog froze on point, lunged, returned tail down. And again. Jimmy stood shuddering with anticipation like the dog, raised his .410, shot. Dan stood tensed beside him, talking to him, willing the little pattern of shot to catch a wing, a back, hell, a tail feather.

As they neared the pickup, the dog took up a last point. The boy stumbled over toward the dog. Dan stood back. Jimmy kicked the bird up himself, followed it, shot, missed. As the cock wheeled off to the right, just at the apex of his rise, the man shot. The bird tumbled, a heap of folded feathers, to the ground. Dan stared helplessly at the spot where the cock had fallen. "I think you winged that one," he said, embarrassed.

"No, I shot behind it."

"We'll try again tomorrow."

"Yeah."

The dog trotted up to his master, the dead bird limp in his mouth, iridescent color against the dog's copper coat and the golden stubble.

"Good boy," Dan said, scratched the dog around the ears and took the bird. He looked uncomfortably at his son. "Here," he tossed the pheasant to the boy. "Need a tail feather for your hat?"

"No."

Jimmy emptied his gun the way his father had shown him, pointed it up, shot it, put it on the rack along the rear window of the pickup.

They drove back down the dirt road, along the ditch. Jimmy held the dead pheasant in his lap, stroking it, studying it, as if the bird knew all the answers.

DEER CAMP

They left for Deer Camp in late August when the wheat was in and the pears were picked and the tomatoes were harvested. It was a pilgrimage, begun with arduous travel, surrounded by hardship and history and tradition. It was the first day off her father took all summer. All summer he left the house before daylight and returned after dark, so tired he could hardly sit up at the table to eat the supper Mother had kept warm for him. All summer he would come home mud-caked from irrigating, grim with worry over the pears, which were the money crop, ripening too fast or too slow. And the price was never good. It seemed to his children that they only half saw him this time of year because he left in the dark before dawn to get the pickers started, and he had turned his headlights on by the time he got home at night. He only half heard them when they spoke to him. Their mother shielded him from them. "Don't bother your dad about that now," she'd say. "He's got too much on his mind." Only the powerful smell of his dirt and grease stained pants and sweaty work shirts, left in a heap on the back porch when he came in at night, a muddy dog smell, a sweet, rotten stench, gave proof to them that he inhabited their lives.

But now, at the end of August, deer hunting season in the Coast Range, they left for Deer Camp, and they would be gone eight days. Father wouldn't miss it. Neither would Uncle Buck. Grandfather had taken the two brothers to Deer Camp when they were boys. The hunting rights had been passed down. Deer Camp was sacred.

The preparations took days. Aunt Helen, her father and uncle's widowed sister, arrived with her three boys the night before to drive up with Uncle Buck. That same night her father loaded the back of the Ford. He wrapped the deer rifles in canvas sleeping bags and laid them in the trunk so there was just room for a covered cake pan with one of Mrs. Decker's hefty German applesauce sheet cakes, plump with raisins and walnuts and smeared with a thick coat of chocolate frosting. Their army duffel bags went in on top to cushion the rifles and the cake. Aunt Helen always made four batches of Aunt Helen's molasses cookies, which were the best cookies in the world, packed in round red tins with roses painted on the lids. Every year Uncle Buck brought a sack of sweet, purple torpedo onions and a sack of white corn. Her father brought a lug of fat beefsteak tomatoes and a lug of ripe pears. They would hunt for meat.

The drive to Deer Camp was seven hours long, and hot. They headed north up the scorched inland valleys of the California Coast Range, and the sun ricocheted back and forth off the old yellow hillsides on either side of them blasting them with heat. By ten o'clock in the morning her shorts and her skinny legs stuck to the back seat, the windows were rolled down, a hot wind blew. She felt carsick.

They drove up highway 101 to Willits, where they always stopped at the creamery for root beer floats, her father's favorite. Then on up to Laytonville, where they always stopped for a block of ice for the icebox. Finally, out of Laytonville, they turned off the highway onto a rough, graveled road headed East. Now the children began to bounce up and down in the back seat singing "She'll be Comin' Round the Mountain When She Comes," and Dad honked the horn, beep! beep! In the course of the trip he was transformed from a shadowy figure back into their dad, their grandfather's son, Uncle Dan's nephew. Now they were almost there.

It was the same each year. They labored up the last hot hill onto Grouse Ridge, squinting in the glare, remarking on the red dirt road, which seemed in worse shape than ever, and the sun-burnt grass, "taller this year, I think. More feed." They recognized every dry creek bed and blazing red manzanita thicket, remembered the year there was a big buck standing right on top of the hill, right out in the sun—a big rack on him. And the smell of Deer Camp came back to her: the sweet, smoky brush, the odor of dry grass and oak leaves.

It was leased land. Grandfather had leased the hunting rights 50 years before, and her dad and Uncle Buck still leased them, seven sections of ancient coast range, Chimney Rock to Red Mountain, a rusted chain and a stubborn padlock on the gate.

And there on a hilltop under a stand of fir trees, a cold spring poured out into an old wood water trough. That was Deer Camp. That was all there was. The spring welled out of a hidden crease. The hillside folded in around it, clothing it with bracken and cress and gold backed ferns. A galvanized pipe had been inserted deep into the spring, and water bubbled out of the pipe into the trough with a greedy, gulping sound. Spring water dripped down the rocks, as well, and oozed out of the ground beneath the pipe so that there was always a damp, soft, muddy place around the spring, always the cool, high, musical pitch of droplets on leaves and the low hollow sound of water on rock. She cupped her hands and drank from the trough, and the water tasted like moss and wet cedar, the way it always did. The old wood felt spongy along the edges. Skaters scooted sideways across the top of the trough, and the water ran out of it down the hillside making little green rivulets in the thirsty dirt.

The equipment was just as they had left it the year before on the leveled-out place beside the spring, covered with tarps—the propane stove, the icebox and the table, the skillet, the tin plates. The iron bedsteads were stacked against the meat safe. But every year the noise of the spring water gurgling into the old trough and spilling out again down the hillside was a surprise to her, and the swish of the afternoon breeze in the fir trees was a surprise, like old melodies that she had learned to hum and then forgotten that she ever knew.

After they unloaded the supplies, each cousin got to choose the tree he wanted to sleep under, and there was some arguing. They drove nails into the trees to hang their flannel shirts, and she wove a bower of fir branches over her cot because she'd gotten it into her head that a leafy bower was a very romantic thing.

The nights cooled off because they were near the coast. The fire that first night in camp blazed just as high as they remembered because her father supervised the building, "Three logs to make a fire. Where's your kindling? Come on now, manzanita kindling for a hot fire. Split your logs." And Mother winced when the boys whacked with the axes. But every man must know how to build a fire.

Immediately after the fire was lit it flamed, blazing a yellow circle, and people settled on this old stump or that camp chair, the canvas patched with gunnysack. Aunt Helen sang a word or two of "Strawberry Roan," starting in the middle, and they sang whatever verse anyone remembered next, helter skelter, so that the song had no beginning or end but ran in a quiet circle around the fire until Mother begged for "The Streets of Laredo," which was her favorite and has so many verses it goes on forever anyway.

Little memories that had attached themselves to the songs or to the fire flickered up. A word or two. "Somebody's been into Aunt Helen's cookies," Mother said.

"Ground squirrels, ground squirrels." Ground squirrels were the scapegoats of Deer Camp.

Her brother Jimmy asked about that wild boar Uncle Buck wounded over by Red Mountain 20 years ago, and then about the cougar who stalked Dad when he was twelve, stories they'd all heard as long as she could remember but begged to hear again, listening not just for the stories but for the teasing and the boyishness as Dad and Uncle Buck outdid each other, watching to see their faces open up into grins, listening for Uncle Buck's soft laughter and her dad's deep chuckle.

There were new stories, too. "Think that old sow is still on the lookout for Jenny?" her father asked, winking at Uncle Buck, because once she'd gotten too close to a wild pig and her piglets, and the sow had chased her up the hill right into camp.

"So, Sam," Uncle Buck would say, "starting another snake collection?" Because last year Aunt Helen had gone down to kiss Sam good night and found a rattlesnake under his cot.

But Sam wasn't going to bed. Nobody was. Her father hadn't recited Robert Service yet. When the fire had burned down just to the point where the logs had broken up into chunks of color, a waning fire that would take another log soon, someone said, "How about 'Dan McGrew'?"

"Or 'The Wild,'" she said, which was her favorite, though all the poems ran together, and the desperate lady that's known as Lou lurked in the shadows of every stanza. Her father hesitated as if waiting for his own father to begin. Grandfather's recitations had been famous. She helped him with the first line,

Have you gazed on naked grandeur . . .
and the virile language summoned blood in a rush to her face.
But her father, with a lick of his lips, smacked into it,

> **. . . where there's nothing else to gaze on,**
> **Set pieces and drop-curtain scenes galore,**
> **Big mountains heaved to heaven, which the**
> **blinding sunsets blazon,**
> **Black canyons where the rapids rip and roar?**

rolled it on his tongue, nearly swallowed in until it filled his
chest and rumbled out of him, deep thunder in the circle of the fire,

> **Have you suffered, starved and triumphed,**
> **groveled down, yet grasped at glory,**
> **Grown bigger in the bigness of the whole?**
> **"Done things" just for the doing, letting babblers**
> **tell the story,**

And though no one moved, no one dared to break the spell, they
fastened themselves closer together around the fire, a head against
Uncle Buck's thigh, a toe against a bigger boot, an arm around thin
shoulder blades. The poetry reverberated with all the power and the
mystery of manhood, and she never tired of hearing it.

The poem went on as long as anyone could remember bits and
pieces of another stanza, tumbled out like boulders in a mountain
stream, any which way. Finally the poem slowed, and her father began
the final stanza, but she was ready for him with lines of other poems,
so the final rumblings of "The Wild" echoed the beginning of,

> **There's a four-pronged buck a-swinging in the**
> **shadow of my cabin,**

The poems were never allowed to die out. They were banked at
last like the fire with a solid line,

> **Sentinels of the stillness, lords of the last lone land?**

And it grew so quiet she could hear the spring pour into the old
trough from deep within the mountain, spilling out again down the
hillside.

Every year each of the cousins progressed along the hunting
stations according to age and responsibility. The women never
hunted. She was a girl, the only girl of all the cousins, but her
father and her uncle didn't hold it against her. All the cousins were

25

lined up every year while Uncle Buck lectured them on handling a rifle and shot his 30-06 into a log at close range—ripping it apart, leaving a repulsive, jagged hole where the bullet came out the other side, so that they would understand what a bullet could do.

They all "dogged" as soon as they were ten. Her father and Uncle Buck sent them into the manzanita scrub, and they crawled through on their hands and knees, scratched and fly-bitten, covered with ticks, banging with sticks to scare the snakes away, throwing rocks, howling, flushing out the deer. When they were eleven they were allowed to walk behind the men carrying the binoculars, walking quietly, learning where to look. At twelve they were allowed to carry unloaded rifles, and if during the whole trip they never pointed the rifle at anybody or let the barrel fall into the dirt, they might be given their own rifles the next year or the year after that.

Through the years each older cousin had gotten his first buck. The year she turned thirteen her brother had gotten his. Christmas of the same year she received her own 30-30, a sleek Winchester with a dark, beautifully figured walnut stock. She cleaned it and polished it a dozen times. She loved to handle it, feel the cool barrel against her cheek. She thought the rich oily smell of Hoppe's #9 solvent was the most intoxicating fragrance in the world. She practiced shooting by the hour against the back levee behind the house. All summer she studied walking quietly. She had read that Indians walked softly by pressing the whole sole of the foot to the ground at once. She dreamed of riding into Deer Camp with her first buck in the back of the jeep. And the women would have heard the shot, way over by Chimney Rock, just one shot, always a good sign. They'd be waiting, hoping for her first buck, and they would run over to the jeep to meet them, "Did you get anything?" And she dreamed they would all say, "No," the way they always did and look disappointed. But the women would look in the back of the jeep, and there would be her trophy, and she would hold up the warm liver in her bloody, dripping bandanna, and her mother and her aunt would look at her turned bright red and then at her father's face, broken apart with smiles. He would put his hand on her shoulder then and tell them in his booming voice, booming and laughing because he was so excited, the adventure of the hunt and how she shot her first buck. His eyes would shine with pride.

And lunch that day would be a celebration. Her uncle would barbecue the liver in her honor, the liver she had gutted out of her first buck, and when they were seated at the long picnic table under the fir trees, he would add to the story, "Tough shot. A good 50 yards, in the shadow . . ." The liver of her first buck. They would all sit on benches at the oilcloth-covered table and concoct luscious salads out of head lettuce and cottage cheese and cucumbers and the beefsteak tomatoes and the purple torpedo onions. There would be whole Tuscan salamis from San Francisco, Monterey Jack so ripe it oozed, sourdough French bread and the grilled liver of her first buck. She must have dreamed that dream a hundred times the summer after she got her 30-30.

Her cousin Sam had shot his first buck over by Chimney Rock, and it had taken four hours to carry it out. Her father and uncle still laughed about fighting their way up the shale dragging the buck and her cousin Sam, too, who was so excited and exhausted he had thrown up. Her brother's buck last year was a fantastic shot. Both her uncle and her father said so. A running shot. They didn't believe he had even grazed it. But they waited and walked down into the draw to check for blood, and there, not a dozen yards from where her brother had shot him, lay the buck behind a toyon, dead, shot right through the chest. She'd never seen her father's face so proud as that day.

Nobody said so, but everybody knew. This was her year to get her first buck. The first three days of hunting were slow. There was a full moon. The deer fed at night, her uncle said. Her father shot a little forked horn on the second morning hunt, so there was meat in camp, but the hunting wasn't good. She began to worry. The third night around the fire her uncle said to her father, "Dan, tomorrow morning you and Jenny better take a walk over to Chimney Rock. The boys and I will go around low and do a little dogging, see if we can't scare something up to you." The boys all groaned. Her father never said a word. She could only see his solid shape hunched on a log outlined against the firelight, but she knew he had looked over at her, and she knew that tomorrow was the day of her first buck.

She didn't hear another song. Her stomach shriveled up and she kept forgetting to breathe. She couldn't sing. She sat beside the fire feeling cold and listening to the spring water pouring into the old trough from deep in the mountain. It seemed that night to drown out all the poetry.

She imagined she wouldn't sleep that night, or that she would dream. But the next thing she knew her father was sitting on the edge of her cot in the dark gently shaking her. The moon shone through the trees above his head. She was wide awake at once, and cold. Her father was excited. She could feel it in his hand on her hair. "Hurry up, now," he whispered, not wanting to wake the women, "we want to be out there at first light. Bring your tags."

Up the hill, in a pool of white light from the Coleman lantern, her uncle fried eggs. She slid in at one end of the table and looked at her egg. Her father and her uncle knew every game trail and buckeye tree in the ten square miles they hunted. They had learned to hunt them with their father. They leaned on the red and white checked oilcloth sipping coffee, talking about the slide below Chimney Rock and the old spring and that clearing where they saw the cat; and she knew that they had seen the mountain lion in that clearing when her father was her age. They planned the hunt, talked with their mouths full, reached for another chunk of venison steak, wiped egg yolk off their tin plates with pieces of burnt toast.

The cousins sat beside her on the benches, spooning strawberry preserves onto their toast and listening. Six cousins all arranged along the bench according to age, an unspoken order. They all had freckles and peeling noses, and they all wore hats—baseball caps, cowboy hats, or billed caps that said **JOHN DEERE TRACTOR** across the front. Hers was a gray, sweat-stained Stetson, a hand-me-down from her uncle. With her ponytail tucked inside the brim, they all looked alike. Except today she was different. She could feel the three younger boys looking up the table at her.

After breakfast they collected their rifles from the rack of lashed poles and pushed the sputtering jeep up the dirt road out of camp. As they headed out, her mom sat up in her sleeping bag and waved. She knew her mom was waving at her. By now the blackness had faded, but still there was no tinge of morning. With headlights on they rattled out to the ridge road. She jumped out and opened the gate. No one even argued about it.

They left the jeep and divided up. Five minutes after they separated, the silent hills folded them in. Shivering with cold and excitement she followed her father along a game trail, around the hill and down into a gully. They climbed the other side of the gully and walked out onto a point. They settled against a manzanita stump with their rifles beside them, and her father lit a cigarette. They never spoke. They waited; She scoured the hillsides until her eyes watered, listening for an uneven rustle in the manzanita brush. Each hunt began something like this. They pretended to be looking for deer, but it was too early. It was their favorite time. They were hunting the dawn. They stalked her, knowing her trails and where she bedded down for the night. They waited and when she came, stampeding pink and orange across a streaked sky, they were amazed. A great gold sun pursued her, burning through the mountain tops. The light kindled the dry flat heat, and a Coast Range day began. They stood up. Her father stubbed his cigarette into the dirt. They went on around the hill toward Chimney Rock. Now they were hunting deer.

But they didn't see a deer all morning. They could hear the boys down in the canyons crashing through the brush, sliding on the shale. The clatter of rock falling. On Chimney Rock nothing stirred. The day grew hot as the end of the morning hunt approached. The yellow grass and the red dirt faded in the midday glare. The landscape looked baked on. Not a bird or a ground squirrel moved. This wasn't the hunt she'd imagined. It was getting too late. The deer flies were bad.

Her uncle and the boys broke out of the brush a hundred yards below them, coated with sweat and orange dust, panting.

"Nothing," her father called.

"Nope," said her uncle. "We kicked up a couple does. That was it. We'll go back down the ridge and get the jeep. Why don't you and Jenny cut along high, take your time. Maybe we'll shake something out."

The boys looked at her as though it were her fault.

They took a deer trail around the open hillside, staying high. Her rifle was heavy on her shoulder. Sweat stung her eyes, smudged her eyeglasses. Where was her buck? She loosed a rock on the trail, and it flipped carelessly, head over tail, down the hill. Her father swung around, irritated. Something had gone wrong. It wasn't turning out the way she'd imagined it. The fury of the sun was catching—angry, grasping heat that seared her skin and sucked out all the juices. The morning dragged on. Even the rattlesnakes and the alligator lizards took cover on these days. Life hid in the shadows and the damp canyon bottoms until the sun crashed into the Coast Range and burned itself out. They wouldn't see a buck this time of day. She'd missed her chance.

She heard a click, her father slipping a cartridge into his chamber. She crept forward, crouching low. Down the gully—maybe forty yards—the buck had heard it, too. He stood motionless under a buckeye, looking in their direction, his body blurring into the fallen buckeye leaves at his feet. Her father stepped aside, and she took his place, sat, braced her elbows on her knees, pumped a shell into the chamber of her rifle, her hands shaking. The buck stood taut, his rack tall and wide.

"Steady, Jen . . ." her father's low, deep voice, "get him in your sights. Steady . . . squeeze . . . now."

She shot. The deer leapt straight into the air and disappeared. Gone. He hadn't run. He'd vanished. No crashing through the brush, no sound at all, except the flies around her ears. She sat resting her elbows on her knees, trembling, looking through her sights at the empty clearing.

"Gut shot. Damn!" A blazing whisper in the sun.

She looked behind her. Gut shot? The cardinal sin of a hunter. If you shot too low or too far back behind the shoulder, the buck was mortally wounded, but he could run for miles before he fell. He suffered horribly. They would have to track him until dark, all the next day if necessary. The meat would be ruined. A careless, wasteful kill. A good hunter never gut shot a buck.

She rested the stock of her rifle on the ground between her shaking knees and leaned her forehead against the hot barrel. Shame pounded through her. Her face burned. "Gut shot?"

"I couldn't tell for sure. I had him in my scope. You were a little low, I think. We'll wait here, give him time."

She clenched her barrel. Sweat rolled down the sides of her face, made her eyes sting. "Three-pointer, Dad?" Her voice cracked.

"Yeah, nice buck. I just hope . . ." He didn't finish the sentence. He was scanning the brush below in the gully with his binoculars. His face was pale and streaked.

The grove of buckeyes below them shimmered in the heat. The fallen leaves around the trees seemed to dance in the mottled shade. The brush behind the buckeyes was a gray-green smear. The harder she looked, the less she could make out.

"O.K., Jen, go slow. You don't want to make him run if you can help it."

She rose and walked down the slope, stalking cautiously toward the clearing. Her father followed, as she knew he would. "Oh, God," she prayed, "please, not gut shot. Let me have missed him clean." She and her brother had lain on their cots at night whispering about what they would do if they accidentally shot a doe. There were comments from time to time about dad's cousin Arthur. He had disobeyed the laws of the hunt somehow. Nobody'd ever said how, and they had never dared to ask. He'd never come back to Deer Camp. "Not gut shot," she prayed.

He wasn't dead. The buck lay in the brown leaves not ten yards from where they'd last seen him, thin legs stretched out. He raised his head. Brown, liquid eyes staring straight at her. She knelt and steadied her rifle aiming at those eyes. No anger there, no terror, but an aliveness. Aliveness quivered in the buck's bright eyes. Even in the suffocating heat, she felt as cold as spring water.

"Shoot," her father whispered, "Don't let him get up. Shoot."

She sighted her rifle.

In all her brash young life she had never seen anything so alive.

She squeezed the trigger gently, gently. Shot.

Permission to reprint portions of **The Call of the Wild, The Rhyme of the Remittance Man,** and **The Pines** from **The Collected Poems of Robert Service** was granted by Dodd, Mead and Company, New York, N.Y. 10016

PATRONA

No birds sing. The pickers are silent, too, the cautious quiet of foreigners in a strange land, the sleepwalking quiet of men at first light. The sun has not yet come up over the levee to touch the tops of the pear trees and bring the orchard to life. It is easy to be the boss at dawn. Even if you are only nineteen you can be the boss at dawn.

I walk the orchard enjoying its various greens: a quiet green dampered by the pear trees, fresh green sprouting from the irrigated earth, green refracted by the dew, green muted by the ripening gold and the soil brown of decay. The early morning light slants, seems to rise from under damp earth, from within wet leaves, each leaf, each blade of grass a moist glaze of green. I walk the rows of pear trees appearing to supervise the pickers, but they are hidden in the leaves. Only their worn out running shoes and their frayed pant cuffs are visible on the upper rungs of their wobbly three-legged ladders. In fact I walk because it is too cold to stand still. My feet are wet. I am the *patrona* in my family orchard. I supervise the greens.

Wild grasses mat the orchard. I do not know their names. Last year at college I learned about Buddhism and William Faulkner and bio-chemistry, but I didn't learn the names of the grasses at my feet: yellow-green grasses with heavy, sleepy heads, broad-leafed grasses to blow through, slim silver-stemmed grasses to suck. Blue-green tufts of wire grass sprout between the lankier grasses, scrambling for space in the sun. Languorous gray-green morning glories wind up through the grasses encircling, strangling. The pear trees wear a somber green, their twisted, hundred-year-old limbs like a dark crowd of upraised arms.

From a little after five in the morning until sometime after seven the orchard is cool and fresh and peaceful. When the pickers stagger up to the bins with their full sacks of pears they speak softly, their faces turned toward their task. The older men's brows are ridged and furrowed by years of hard labor in the fields and orchards. Their lips are cracked. The young men have the smooth cheeks of children, although they have sworn to be eighteen years of age. Their young lashes still hide lively eyes.

"Buenos dias, Patrona."

"Buenos dias, Julio."

"Como está, Ruiz?"

They empty the seventy pound picking sacks strapped to their chests quickly, gently, a muffled rumble in the bottom of the wooden bins, then run off, racing the heat that will smother the orchard by midday.

I form a question in my mind. I want to ask Julio about his little girl, his second child, who cut her arm on barbed wire. I wonder if she had a tetanus shot. This is difficult. I do not know how to say "tetanus shot" in Spanish. I rehearse the question. When Julio comes back with his next sack, I ask him.

"Five stitches," he says. "Ah yes, the tetanus."

It is the same word.

"Yes she had the tetanus. All goes well with her. *Gracias, Patrona."* He smiles, and his face lights suddenly in the shadows. He hurries off.

The trees are good in this block. The picking goes well. I hear the sun in the tree tops before I feel it on the orchard floor. First, the birds—the long flute song of the finches and the violet swallows, then the bugle call of a blackbird atop a cattail in the full irrigation ditch that borders the orchard. The men begin to call to one another in the trees. Tomas's dark voice floats down out of the treetops, a murky, liquid melody, perhaps a love song. The words are slurred by the dialect, muffled by the trees. I do not understand the words. The tune echoes in my head. The other pickers cheer him and join in on the refrain. They begin to tease one another, speaking rapidly, laughing. Sometimes I catch the meaning. The old man, Ruiz—they call to him:

"Ruiz, you are slowing down. Shall we send a wheelchair to help you bring your sack in, Ruiz?"

"Better we send an ambulance, Ruiz."

Sometimes I do not understand the joke. I do not ask. I keep my Spanish dictionary in my back jeans pocket, but the words I need are never there.

The crew boss, Don Angel, helps me with my Spanish, speaks slowly, distinctly to me, corrects me, teaches me new words. He first came to the orchards the summer I was eleven. But when I went away to college last fall, I forgot everything. He pronounces my name Jennifer with a soft H sound.

"Paciencia, Hennifer,*"* he says. "It will come back, *Patronita."*

But when he wants to speak to the men so that I cannot understand, he speaks a language he has never taught me.

It is not a language for women
It is not a language for *Anglos.*
It is not a language for bosses.
I am triply foreign.

The morning turns golden. Sun gilds the highest leaves and lights the spider webs in the grasses. The men smile, warm, easy smiles kindled in their eyes. Faded flannel shirts and ragged jackets come off, left at the ends of the rows. Ruiz brings me a gift, an empty bird nest he has found in the tree tops. I sip hot coffee from my thermos. My feet are warming up. We should pick forty bins today at this rate.

"Mas peras, Senores." Don Angel sings out to the pickers. He walks up straight and tall in a pressed shirt and Levis. His black hair is close-cropped; his eyes are full of dark intelligence. More pears. He calls out to the men by name.

I know their names. Their names are not easy. Twenty-four men, three picking crews. They are all related, and the names on their papers are often false names, so one must learn the names by ear. The relationships are complicated. Half-brothers and cousins and uncles and sons-in-law. Their Social Security numbers vary from season to season. *"Hola, Tomas."* Tomas is the nephew of Don Angel. He is a school teacher in Guanajuato.

At ten o'clock Don Angel goes for the men's lunches, which Mama Lola fixes at the labor camp—tortillas and beans, pickled vegetables so delicious that I often take one, so full of hot peppers that my mouth burns for the rest of the day. My mouth is not a Mexican mouth. Mama Lola is Don Angel's wife, a face as brown and smooth as a clay pot. She stays at the camp. She does not come into the orchard. Don Angel has never said to me the orchard is no place for a woman. After all, my father, his good friend, has only two sons. One son has left the land to become an attorney. The younger son is away in Australia learning about orchards. I need a summer job. There are other crops. My father cannot be everywhere. My father speaks no Spanish. He and Angel communicate perfectly.

Don Angel returns with the lunches, and I detect a quickening in the trees. Don Angel is back in the orchard. I call out to watch for soft fruit, which will rot rather than ripen. *Madura* is the word for soft fruit. There is no answer. I do not know if the pickers have even heard me. They have stopped talking.

Tomas calls out to Don Angel, teasing him about the lunches, about Mama Lola. Deep *chu* sounds and harsh *hu* sounds turn the language husky, masculine. The men laugh at Tomas and at Angel's retort. I busy myself with packout slips, jotting in the notebook I carry in my shirt pocket, figuring. I am supposed to be *patrona*.

By one o'clock the light is white. It flattens the trees, wilts the grasses, presses against the back of the neck. We are into a block of young trees, and the patches of shade are small, spotty. The picking slows. There is more limb rub in this block. Sweat stains the pickers' shirts and runs down their faces as they lug their full sacks over to the bins. Their smiles are still generous, the smiles they give to children. I try to chat with them, but I am running out of cheerful things to say in Spanish. My back aches from bending over the waist-high bins to sort the bruised and damaged fruit that will be rejected by the cannery. My hands are filthy, my fingernails black and broken. My blue chambray work shirt is stuck to my back. I straighten up and go for a drink of water at the water cooler on the pear bin trailer.

Tomas comes up to the water cooler, talking to Julio. They are arguing, their voices tired, irritated. I reach for a cup of water, wishing Tomas would shut up, for heaven's sake. Tomas is a loud mouth. Sweet rot of fermenting fruit rises from the orchard floor. The fruit flies are terrible.

Suddenly their voices crack, loud, harsh. Julio lunges for Tomas. Tomas whirls, locks Julio's arms. The stifling afternoon explodes—a thousand shafts of sunburnt anger. I drop my paper cup. My high school Spanish dries in my throat. What is happening? What sparked the fight? Two fiery egos glisten with sweat, rear up in the sun. They wrestle savagely now. The pickers materialize from the trees and watch silently, unsurprised. They have seen it coming. Only I am taken by surprise.

Stop. Do not kill one another. Dear God, please, no knives, I pray, but silently. "Do not kill" involves the imperative. "No knives," the subjunctive. My mouth is open, but it is shock, not language. I stand speechless, squinting into the sun.

They back off a step, hurling words at one another, not the language they speak to me, that polite baby talk. This is a guttural growl of hate and pride. A knife blade glints. I see a shirt sleeve tear.

Don Angel barks, rushes forward, barks at them again, a word I do not know. The men pause, separate, turn their backs on one another, muttering over their shoulders. The pickers give them room.

Don Angel says, "Not here, not now," the first words I have understood. There is another silence.

"Mas peras," Don Angel says, turning to the pickers. "We need more pears." The pickers back slowly into the white hot orchard. They glance at me.

"Dos mas," I call out. Two more bins. But my voice is nearly a screech. My legs tremble. "Only two more," I try again. I straighten up and walk the bleached rows, looking up at the backs of the silent pickers. I do not know what the fight was about. I did not see it coming. I do not know if it is really over.

I do not speak the language.

I do not even comprehend the silences.

THE SEÑORA'S GARDEN

At first she only weeds them, the flowers in the Señora's garden. The tough horsehair roots of the crabgrass must be dug out with a sharp shovel. The Senora's house is the largest house in the town. Her garden is the most beautiful garden. Lupe loves the garden, even on the days when the north wind snaps at her, and the Señora says, "No, Lupe, it is too cold for you outside. Dust the bookcases." The wind makes even the birds fly like crazy things, sideways across the sky. To Lupe it is nothing. Along the paths little white bells reach up out of a deep V of leaves, delicate green-tipped bells that the angels would envy. They nod to her as she walks the garden paths. The Señora's garden grows nothing to eat, no corn, no peppers. Only flowers. It is a feast for the eye. Then the little blue flowers begin to swarm the garden in clouds. "Forget-me-nots," the Señora calls them, *"Non olvidarme."* With yellow eyes. She divides them for the Señora, and they wander about the garden like lost souls. The first rose petals are the tender pink of a baby's ear lobe. The fat thorns are like the sharp wail of a hungry infant. They only make the little buds seem more fragile.

One day the Señora needs flowers for her dinner party. "Please, Lupe, go to the cutting garden," she says. "Cut me flowers, and put them in deep water, please."

The cutting garden is a paradise. It is not a prisoner of the green lawn and the brick path. It dances out behind the hedge, sneaks around the potting shed, climbs the back fence. Here the birds come to drink from the basin Lupe leaves beside the faucet, and the field mice come to have their babies in the straw bales behind the shed. Lupe loves to go to the cutting garden. And oh, how she cuts. In half an hour her bucket is washed in pinks and purples, crabapple blossoms and quince and the fire-orange of the last tulips, all spilling from the bucket.

The Señora looks at the bucket for a long time, and she smiles, "You have an eye, Lupe. You have a sense of color."

Oh, glorious Señora. She is proud of her own flower bouquets, but from that day she always asks Lupe to arrange a few flowers for her.

"Please, Lupe, a little bouquet on the butler's tray," she says. "Please, a vase on the library table."

During her working hours! It is the happiness of nursing a baby when one has full breasts. To wander in the cutting garden in the early morning, before the ladybirds are awake, gathering armfuls of flowers: the heartbreaking pinks of the roses, the camellias, the party-dress colors of the sweet peas. She learns all their names. She, who cannot tell between the silver polish and the brass polish, she learns every one by heart. The perfume of the stock and the lavender. She closes her eyes and crushes them to her bosom. She strokes the rose petals, the soft silk petals, and sticks her nose into their sweet faces, breathing in their scent.

Once, when the Señora goes away with her husband the banker on a trip, she says, "You must cut the flowers while I am gone, Lupe, and take them home. They will stop blooming if you do not encourage them."

And Lupe cuts. All around her poor house in mayonnaise jars, on the shelf, on the toilet tank, the flowers make the room look like a church, like a garden. On the sink, on lug boxes. The chipped linoleum floor does not matter so much with jars of flowers on it. The poor, wrecked walls are not so bad. She sits at the table in her house in the tipping chair, but she does not notice that the chair tips or that the faucet in the sink is dripping, dripping. The flies circle the room. There is a hole in the window screen. But it is of no importance. Alfonzo is not home yet, yelling for his dinner, his *cerveza*. She sits in her house, and the roses come to her in crushed, velvet colors, yellows and pinks and red. Only blood could be so deep a red, she thinks. She is content.

Alfonzo does not always come home to her. He makes no secret that he lusts for her younger sister, Gloria, who lives with her aunt. He blames Lupe. He says her babies die, which is true. God have mercy. And Gloria does not discourage him enough. Gloria, round and smooth as a camellia. She is not brown at the edges. She has not dried up and faded yet. Even Lupe loves to look at her.

Each day she goes to the house of the Señora. But more and more she works in the garden. In the house she breaks things. Her fingers are too big for the brittle little cups. They squirm out of her hands and fall. She stands in the Señora's pantry and looks at the shattered cup lying on the floor like a dead thing, and tears come to her eyes.

"Never mind, Lupe," the Señora says. "I will wash the cups and the wine glasses. I need you in the garden. The flowers need you."

She digs like a mad one in the garden. The dirt of the Sacramento Delta is black and thick. She chases the weeds until they take cover in the lawns. They are afraid to return to the flower beds. She cuts away the wilted rose blossoms that climb the fences, leaving the fresh rosebuds to bloom. She feeds the flowers with the fish liquid to make them strong.

"You stink like a dead catfish," Alfonzo says.

It is hard to wash the smell away, but her young flowers grow new shoots. Strong, husky zinnias leap from the ground. Their stems are thick and hairy. Delphiniums and hollyhocks stand tall as corn. Petunias and lobelias ruffle all the borders like petticoats. The morning glory overrunning the potting shed is a *rebozo* of blue blossoms.

The Señora says, "Lupe, the garden has never looked so healthy. You are a good gardener."

Sometimes she does not want to go home. There is a wood crate in the cutting garden beside the lavender. Sometimes she thinks she will go sit on this crate and watch the moon come up.

This is a green, plentiful valley. Always there is water. The river winds through it. The ditches are full. In the garden water leaps from the hose at the touch of a hand. One need never carry water or save it to wash one thing and then another. Alfonzo does not like this valley. He longs for Mexico. He says it is wet and cold and cruel in this valley. He says it is dangerous. He has a gun, which is a foolish thing. He keeps it in his truck, but he forgets to lock the truck. The children in the next house could easily find it. All men carry guns, he says. The Señora's husband has a gun.

"Yes," Lupe says, "but he uses it only in winter." In the winter he shoots the ducks who fly past in a long, wavering line, hoping to reach Mexico.

"You see!" says Alfonzo.

Something attacks the penstemon, the lovely little penstemon with pink and yellow newborn faces. They are thick in the flower beds, surrounding the blue salvia, jostling the godetia. Suddenly their leaves droop, and they turn pale. She runs to the Señora.

"Señora, the flowers are very sick. Please come quickly."

When the Señora's husband comes home from the bank at lunchtime, they show him. He pulls one of the wilted plants out of the ground, and there are no roots under it.

"Is it the gopher, Señor?"

"I think it might be a fungus, one of those root-rot things. I'll ask the fertilizer guy when I see him next week."

Next week!

The flowers begin to die. She waters them in the morning and again at night. She feeds them extra fish liquid, but they are too sick to notice. Alfonzo does not come home for two nights. She knows where he is. Each day the flowers grow weaker. Each day the disease spreads. She shows the Señora, but she is busy. Her son and his wife are coming to visit. She needs Lupe to iron, to change the beds, to wax the floors. Lupe has no time to tend her sick flowers. Will the roses get this sickness? Holy Mary, save the roses.

One night when Alfonzo is gone she goes back to the garden in the dark and sits on the box in the cutting garden. The dogs know her. They do not bark. No one can see her behind the hedges. She dozes in the garden. It is still warm. She can still smell the lavender. She prays for the roses.

After a while she gets stiff, so she walks home. Alfonzo's truck is there. Gloria has exhausted him perhaps. Perhaps he is too drunk to satisfy her. He is as rotten as the rotting thing that kills her flowers. She reaches in his truck and gets his gun. She will warn him to stay away from Gloria. The gun is heavy, hard to hold up.

She looks at it. It is an ugly thing. She holds it away from her like a fat, dead rat.

But Alfonzo is too drunk. "Whore," he shouts when she comes in. "Whore. You have been out whoring behind my back. Creeping in at midnight. Slut."

"But, no . . ." she says.

He sees the gun. "And now you come to kill me so you can go off whoring again. You piece of filth."

He is too drunk. She must get out of here, or he will beat her badly. He lunges for her and falls. She stops. She is so surprised. She stops and looks down at him. The gun is hanging from her hand.

"No, you are wrong," she says. "I was with my little flowers."

But she should not have stopped. She should have run. He grabs at the gun, and she fights him off. He hits her hard across the mouth and grabs again.

And then she sees only red, the red of roses on her eyelids. She opens her eyes, and she sees only the crushed, velvet red. Holy Mother, only roses could be so deep a red.

GALLITO

John brushed past the lush clumps of cilantro growing beside the cookhouse door. ("The spices in this country are stale," Mama Lola said. "They taste like old hay.") The green cilantro made John's nose wrinkle, made him hungry. When he opened the screen door, Mama Lola turned and smiled at him. Her smooth, round face was wreathed with a black braid twisted across the top of her head. She wore a freshly ironed apron sewn from a flour sack. "Hungry already, Juanito?" she ruffled his red hair. "Wash your hands at the sink, and we will see." Mama Lola stood before her mammoth black stove stirring bubbling pots on heavy claw-like burners, black beans and *menudos* and mysterious dark chocolate *moles.* Above the stove on a warming shelf, wrapped in a clean dishtowel, Mama Lola always kept a few hand-made flour tortillas, thin, delicate as butterfly wings.

Mama Lola's cookhouse, a two story wood frame building that leaned toward the river, stood at the edge of the orchard. Outside the paint was blistered and peeling, but inside the walls were freshly painted every year so that now, after so many years, the walls and woodwork looked like they had been coated with vanilla icing. The faded linoleum was waxed, glossy. Mama Lola insisted on it.

John sat at one of the long oilcloth covered tables lined with chili salsa bottles, napkin holders and jam jars filled with pink oleander blossoms. He chewed quietly on his tortilla and studied the bright flower pattern on the red oilcloth. Mama Lola brought the oilcloth from Mexico, along with all the spices for her cooking, her dried chiles, her epazote, her oregano, her vanilla. She grew her own cilantro.

John was a quiet, serious boy of twelve. He'd been sent up from a nice suburb of San Francisco to work for his Uncle Rob for a month during pear season, while his friends spent the summer swimming or water skiing at Lake Tahoe. His father had worked in this same orchard with his father. He didn't want John hanging around the country club swimming pool all summer, so John was sent to live with his grandparents for pear season. His grandmother plied him with angel food cakes and berry pies and fussed over him when he dragged in every afternoon hot and dirty and tired from the orchard.

"You poor thing," his grandmother would say. "It's 102 today, the radio says. What's your Uncle Rob thinking," she clucked, "keeping you out there in this heat." All the while pouring fresh, icy lemonade, handing him a plate of tollhouse cookies.

But Uncle Rob would be out in front the next morning at four thirty, and John would stumble sleepily into his pickup clutching a sack with a half dozen cookies and the three peanut butter and apricot jam sandwiches his grandmother had made for him the night before. By 8:00 he had eaten all his cookies. By 9:30 he had eaten all his sandwiches. He was starving.

"¿Como estás? How goes it, Juanito?" Mama Lola asked. "Is it hot out there yet?"

John nodded, his mouth full. Mama Lola had sprinkled his tortilla with sugar and cinnamon. He had been sent from the orchard to get his Crew Three's lunches, but he hated to leave Mama Lola's quiet kitchen. Later, when the men came into the cookhouse for dinner at 4:00, they all must be showered and in clean shirts. No drinking and no swearing in her cook house. No whores or drugs in the camp. No walking into town for beer. Those were Mama Lola's rules, and the men obeyed them. She watched closely out her window when vans pulled into the camp, keeping a lookout for Immigration, *La Migra*. John had seen vans of women pull into the camp too, women with big bellies and breasts spilling out of their tight pants and skimpy tops. He'd watched Mama Lola march out of the cookhouse, spoon in hand, and send them off.

Mama Lola was married to Angel, the crew boss, and besides she was a great cook, as good as his grandmother, John thought.

John's job was to drive the tractor through the orchard slowly, keeping up with a picking crew so they could empty their picking sacks into the five four-foot-square wood bins on his trailer. At first he had been excited about driving a tractor. His friends in sixth grade thought it was cool. But it turned out to be harder than he thought. His tractor was an old Farmall with a crank start that nearly broke his pipestem arms every morning as he struggled to start it. Uncle Rob had removed second and third gear from the tractor after some bad experiences with sixteen-year-old tractor drivers, so John could only drive at a crawl. Rob had made him practice in the yard for a week before pear season, maneuvering between buckets. Still, trailers were tricky. Yesterday John had turned a corner too sharply and wedged the trailer between two pear trees. Angel, the crew boss, had had to use a forklift to get it unstuck.

"Juanito, you were not thinking, not paying attention," Angel had said sternly. "You have cost your Crew Three much time and much money. You must have a care for your crew."

It was true that Crew Three had been surly with him for the rest of the day—no teasing, no calling him by his nickname, *Gallito,* no teaching him dirty words in Spanish. Even this morning they ignored him when they came back to the trailer to dump their sacks of pears. Jose had knocked him aside without a word. No *"Buenos dias, Gallito,"* no *"Marmota"* (sleepy-head.) He had to get back out into the orchard by 10:00 with their lunches or they would be mad at him all over again. They ate their lunches promptly at 10:00. It seemed he couldn't do anything right.

"So Juanito, here you go," said Mama Lola. "All the lunches. Yours too. And two more tortillas for your pocket. Have a care. They are hot."

Rob watched John trudge back with the box of lunches for Crew Three. The kid looked listless, bedraggled. Yesterday had been a disaster. John was too young to drive tractor. He was a good kid, with crooked front teeth that would require braces and feet so big they were constantly tripping him up, but he didn't have the judgment yet. Rob had been crazy to agree to hire his brother Jim's son for the summer. He had enough problems with Crew Three as it was.

It was Rob's own fault. He had badly underestimated the crop, and Angel had had to round up a third crew at the last minute, all illegal probably. They had faked Social Security numbers and phony papers. There were three "Jorge Valdezes" on the payroll already, and half the men used the same address in Stockton, some P.O. Box number. The payroll was a nightmare to him. He worked late every night at his father's heavy old desk, still full of crumbs of pipe tobacco and the hard butterscotch candies his father loved. Every night he swatted mosquitoes drawn to the desk lamp and tried to sort out the payroll, trying to post the pickers' pay correctly, to deduct the withholding that most of the men would never get, trying to learn their names, which turned out to be false. They didn't even answer to them.

The other two picking crews were mostly legal, "green cards" or Chicanos who had come up years ago and would somehow show up every pear season. A few of them he had known ten years ago when he drove tractor for his dad during his summer vacations in high school. They came up from Tecate or Pascualitos in banged-up Chevrolets with one fender gray, one yellow. They started picking in the south, Imperial Valley, working their way north: asparagus, cherries, peaches, pears . . . . Sometimes stopping off after picking the grapes to prune the orchards in October before going home to Mexico. Some of the men had managed to get their families up and lived in Stockton now. They had finagled their kids into Head Start programs, spoke some English if they had to.

Each crew was paid by the number of bins it picked, and Crew One chose its own pickers. They were the elite. Crew One ran up their tall three-legged ladders, then staggered back to their trailer, knees buckling, lugging seventy pounds of pears strapped to their stomachs. When they unsnapped the bottoms of their pear sacks and eased the pears out into the bins, Rob would find every pear large, unblemished, not punctured by the stems of other pears. The eight men of Crew One could pick 70,000 pounds a day.

Even Crew Two was good. Younger, less serious than Crew One, they sang and called each other names, crazy nicknames: The

Giant, Big Feet. If a picker lagged behind he was dubbed *Chicle,* Chewing Gum. John was named *Gallito,* little rooster, which Rob figured probably had dirty connotations. He never knew. They were a mix of boys only a few years older than John and a few aging pickers who could no longer keep up the pace of Crew One. They could pick, they knew the orchard, and they worked hard.

But this new crew, Crew Three. They were all wild and green. Rob could hear them now banging their aluminum ladders as they moved them, breaking branches. They would be trouble, this Crew Three. If the Immigration *La Migra* came, and they were overdue to raid his orchard, he would have a mess on his hands, now when the fruit was ripening too fast and every hour counted. The price was sinking daily.

Crew Three finished their lunches and came for one last drink of ice water from the tin cup chained to the water cooler on the back of John's trailer, John climbed wearily up onto the tractor. Uncle Rob and Angel came down the row toward him talking quietly.

"The fruit is getting too soft," said Uncle Rob. "We've already had one load rejected. We can't stop picking now. If I give them a day off, they will get drunk, go into town and get mixed up with *La Migra.*"

"And if you don't give them a day off, they will get drunk and head to Washington for the apples. Either way it is the same," said Angel.

"If *La Migra* comes we're finished," said Uncle Rob. "I've heard that they were on Ryer Island yesterday."

"As for *La Migra* . . ." They turned away and lowered their voices.

"I don't know," Uncle Rob said. "That barn's dangerous." Angel looked thoughtfully over at John, who pretended to be busy sorting fruit in his five bins, rolling the pears gently with the palms of his hands, looking for soft pears or stem puncture or limb rub.

"The floor boards up there are rotted. He's clumsy. I don't think it's a good idea."

"Yes, but Juanito is the only one who could do it." Angel turned to John, "Do you think you could climb to the rafters of the old barn? You would have to be cautious, *Gallito*. The floor is very bad."

"What about my crew? Crew Three?" John asked. Was he being fired from his tractor job?

"I would have to take your place," Angel said. "Temporarily," he added. "But this is a more important job right now. It is dangerous, but it is vital."

Angel explained his plan and held the ladder while John climbed up into the rafters with a bent toy bugle in one hand and a water bottle stuffed in his T-shirt. "*Cuidado*, Juanito, careful. The ladder has rotten places. Now you must be vigilant. Do you understand? The pickers are depending on you."

Clutching the rungs of the ladder with his right hand he began climbing, dizzy with the heat, feeling a couple of the rungs give way under his work boots. Getting down would be harder than getting up.

Uncle Rob stood at the bottom of the ladder looking grim. "Watch what you're doing," he said. "It's dangerous up there."

At the top of the ladder John reached for a rafter and took a step across the floorboards. The first step was O.K., but the second board was soft. It gave way when he stepped on it, and the third board had a gaping hole. He clung to the rafters and worked his way slowly to the open end of the barn, sweating, testing the floor, avoiding the dark spots on the floorboards, trying not to look down at the floor of the barn far below him. A pigeon flared up, startling him. Disturbed from its perch in the eaves, it flew in circles around the loft.

John sat in the rotting rafters at the open end of the barn for two long hours looking down over the tops of the pear trees and, beyond the orchards, to the checkerboard of green tomato fields striped with damp dirt between the rows. Beyond the tomato fields he could see the pale green corn in the middle of the island. He scanned the empty road that ringed the island's levee. He picked splinters from the rotten ladder out of his hands. Angel and Uncle Rob had left the barn. He was alone. They just wanted to get rid of me because I'm no good driving tractor, John thought. I wish they'd just fire me so I could go home. He'd heard Uncle Rob say that half of Crew Three was probably illegal. Was what he was doing illegal too? How was he going to get down without falling? It was hard to move perched up in the rafters, and he was getting stiff and drowsy. He was hungry again.

Suddenly, a mile away, three pale green vans rumbled along the levee road. Immigration, *La Migra.* Angel had been right. John grabbed his dented toy bugle and blew a loud, sputtering blast out over the orchard. Three blasts, Angel had said. He blew and blew again. The sound cracked on the high notes, like his own voice lately, but it was loud. The men had heard it. He watched them dash out of the orchard and turn for the cornfields in the middle of the island, crouching low. They disappeared among the tall waving rows of tasseled corn. He eased his way across the floor watching for rotten boards, tripping once, stubbing his toe on a bent nail. Then he worked his way down the ladder, wobbly now without Angel to steady it. He got to the door of the barn in time to see one of the Immigration vans turn down the driveway into the orchard. When the van came into the yard, John started to sprint down the road away from the cornfield, but his legs were stiff and cramped from crouching in the rafters. He pretended he had a limp. That was his own idea, and he was proud of it.

Two uniformed men jumped out of the van. "Stop," one shouted. "Stop. You're under arrest."

John didn't turn around. He ran, as Angel had instructed him, headed for the orchard. The blast of a shotgun exploded in his ears. They were shooting at him! He ducked, glanced over his shoulder, and in that moment he tripped on a dirt clod and fell sprawling onto the road. He looked up to find that the fat man was still pointing a shotgun carelessly in his direction. The man's shirt buttons strained to close across his chest, and his belly spilled over the top of his belt. Was there a handgun there too under that huge gut? John had gotten dirt in his eye. He couldn't tell for sure.

Both men approached John with the shotgun aimed right at him. Then, as they neared him, John could see behind their mirrored sunglasses their expressions begin to change from triumph to pure disgust. John's baseball cap had fallen off. The shock of red hair, his freckled nose, his blue eyes began to register with them. Still they didn't lower the gun. A chill ran down John's spine. He could see men shackled in the back of the van. They looked hot and scared.

"Shit," said the pale man, and he spat into the dust.

"You're obstructing justice, ya' know," said the fat man, his face growing redder. "That's against the law." He lowered the gun sloppily, with the barrel nearly in the dirt. The gun didn't look like John's dad's twelve gauge, which was Italian and had a dark polished stock and a long gleaming barrel. This gun had a stubby barrel and a dark, ugly stock. It looked dirty, dangerous.

Uncle Rob's pickup wheeled into the yard. Having heard the shot and seen John sprawled in the dust, he leapt out and ran to his side. He knelt down and put a hand on his shoulder. "You O.K.?"

"Yeah, I tripped," John mumbled embarrassed.

Rob's terror turned to rage. He looked up at the men, his hand still resting on John's shoulder, "You bastards," he growled.

"Hey, we just fired a warning shot," snapped the pale man. But he backed up a step. His boots were scuffed. There were grease stains down the front of his pants. "He was resisting arrest."

"A twelve-year-old kid?"

John got to his feet, and Uncle Rob put his arm around John's shoulder. John wondered if they were going to arrest him or just shoot him. He tried hard to keep his legs from shaking. In the middle of the road, the sun beat down on them. No one spoke.

"We heard you had a crew of wetbacks out here."

"Look around if you have to, but put that goddamned gun away. We gave the men the rest of the day off. They were tired," Uncle Rob said. "And don't you ever shoot at my nephew again," he added coldly.

The men stared angrily at Uncle Rob and at the ladders still in the trees and the trailers full of pears still idling in the orchard. Uncle Rob stood very straight, feet planted solidly on the dirt road, and met their stares.

John concentrated on his shaking legs.

Finally the red-faced fat man wiped away the sweat streaming down his face and turned, "Let's get out of here. It's too late anyhow. We'll never catch the buggers now." He looked at Uncle Rob. "We'll be back. Don't think we won't."

They got into their van, put the gun back in the gun rack and slammed the doors. They wheeled around and roared back up the driveway onto the levee road, driving too fast, raising dust in the orchard, which was not allowed. Uncle Rob watched them until they were out of sight. Then his face lit up. All the worry and tiredness seemed to slip off his shoulders. He laughed out loud and hugged John hard, "Good work," he said. "Two more hours of picking, and I'm treating for chocolate sundaes at Freddy's Fountain."

Behind him, out in the cornfield, John heard a chorus of whoops and laughter. Then a loud cheer went up. *"Gallito! Gallito! Gallito!"*

HEAT RISES

At lunch she sat in the shade of a wide fig tree beside the river, wishing she had time to take off her work boots and wade. She sat on a spot packed hard by the feet of fishermen. A thin, discarded fishing line floated in the weeds beside her. She thought she might tie the fishing line to her toe and just stay here for the afternoon. A breeze dallied on the surface of the river, but it was a lazy, good-for-nothing breeze, unlikely to climb up over the levee to the packing shed on the inland side. Jen figured no breeze would blow in the shed this afternoon. She closed her eyes and listened to the sway of the cottonwoods above her, the quiet current of the river, the rattle of tules, the hum of a dragonfly.

She didn't need to look at her watch. Lunch hour was nearly over. She rose. The afternoon would be a scorcher. And, of course, she wore too many clothes: long khaki pants because long pants were required at the packing shed; a long-sleeved chambray shirt outside her pants because the Mexican women she employed disapproved of bare arms and tucked-in shirts. She'd spent the morning in hand-to-hand combat with the rollers of the dump elevator, and she had the grease stains to prove it.

The packing shed, on the other side of the levee, was an open steel structure roofed in tin, anchored to a concrete slab. Not that it was likely to go anywhere, Jen thought. Too square and unimaginative. It had no walls, but pear orchards hemmed it in, smothering any breeze. She climbed up onto the metal scaffold walkway to ring the warning bell, so Tom could start the elevator belt that carried the pears out of the water dump and up to the sorters' tables ten feet above the floor of the packing shed. The temperature up here was several degrees hotter still. Heat rises. From the high walkway she looked down on the fruit packers below waiting for the first fruit to be carried along a moving belt from the sorters' tables.

Tom pushed the buttons on the control panel. The machinery clattered to life. The rollers and belts rumbled into action. A mechanical din filled the shed. Poor old, disgusting, alcoholic Tom. Sweat ran in furrows down the stubble on his pebbled face. He looked like a badly plowed field. When she wasn't paying attention, he'd try to speed up the belts, damn him, to get through today's pack sooner, because it was too hot, because he needed a drink, because that's the way they did it in the Northwest, where he'd drifted down from, where he claimed he'd run big packing sheds, ten times bigger than this one. Jen doubted it. But that's what they got here on the backwaters of the Sacramento River, where the work was seasonal and the sheds were small, and all the machinery was secondhand and held together with bailing wire and duct tape.

The sorters already stood at the sorting belt, four women to a side, inspecting the fruit that rolled past them at dizzying, sickening speed. Jen sorted with them for a while, chatting with the women in her simple-minded Spanish. The key to a good-looking box of fruit was the sorters. Consuela's daughter, who used to work beside her mother at the sorting table, now had a job at a pizza parlor in Sacramento (air-conditioning, Consuela said) and was going to Sacramento City Junior College. "Air conditioning." The very words made the women push their lower lips out and exhale softly, "Poof. Air conditioning. *Figurate.*" Imagine. Consuela talked proudly and rapidly in Spanish of her daughter, over the clatter of the machinery, over the waves of heat, and Jen caught about half of what she said. Consuela was a tall, thin woman with an angular face. A black braid, thick and heavy as a gopher snake, hung down her back. She was strong and steady, but she had a temper.

Tom's first mistake in the shed had been to cross Consuela. He'd turned up the machinery too fast, and when the sorters couldn't cull out all the bad fruit, he'd said, "If these cows are too slow, we'll find us some women who ain't."

Consuela had swung her braid like a bullwhip and said in English, "Nobody call me cow." Jen hadn't even known she spoke English. These women had a real nose for bigots. It had taken Jen two days to calm Consuela down.

Jen had waylayed Tom out behind the empty bins and let him have it. "That's red-neck talk, Tom. I won't have it in my shed."

"They take advantage of you, Jen. You got to know how to handle 'em." He'd turned to walk off.

She'd knocked a stack of empty boxes over. In the noise of the shed, it took a real crash to get anybody's attention. She wrecked a couple of boxes, but she made him jump, "They're proud women, and they're hard workers, God dammit. They've been here a lot longer than you have, most of them, and they work for me. Is that clear?"

Jen knew damned well it wasn't clear, that it would go on all season, this simmering feud. It was the kind of thing that kept everybody stirred up all summer, her own personal soap opera. She'd just have to keep an eye out for the next episode.

When Jen climbed down from the sorting table the floor of the shed seemed to sway under her. The sickening motion of the fruit rushing past always made her dizzy. Like stepping off a boat after hours on the river. Jen held the rail and waited for the floor to steady itself. How could those women stand there for eight hours a day? In this suffocating heat? At night Jen had seasick nightmares of the pears rolling past her on the belt, always moving, every pear punctured and bruised, going too fast, crashing, clattering away from her before she could catch it.

Sometimes Jen thought her queasiness might be morning sickness, hoped it might be, but when she got down off the sorting belt, the sick feeling always went away. Jen was wary of dizziness, of falling or catching her hand in the machinery. She had always been clumsy. If she hurt herself her father might think she shouldn't run the packing shed.

Her mother worried about her, looked at her anxiously when she stopped by, "You shouldn't be working so hard when you're trying to get pregnant." Her mother stood in her flower beds with her clippers and her watering can. Jen could see her clipper hand itching when she looked at Jen's wild hair and her sunburned face. Jen could feel her mentally trimming Jen up as if she were a wayward dahlia, applying a little lipstick. "No wonder . . . ." her mother said, and then hesitated to say more. She knew it was a touchy subject.

It hadn't been as easy as Jen thought it would be. Two biology majors. What the hell? She and David had planned to have their first child this winter. Winter is a good time for babies in a farm community. Nobody is quite so busy. But she'd had two early miscarriages. Maybe. A missed period then a sudden flow, cramps. Nobody quite sure. She'd thought pregnancy would be more scientific than this. Or more romantic. One or the other. Her gynecologist was unconcerned. "Don't rush it," the doctor had said. "It will happen." But it was already August.

Jen wasn't panicking. They probably both needed to work another season anyhow. She and David had bought an old Victorian house on Steamboat Slough, and David was just starting out as an Ag Extension field man for the county. They had plenty of time for children. Still, the failure of her own physical machinery seemed to her linked somehow to the breakdowns at the packing shed, the bad belts, the blown fuses, the jammed rollers. It was discouraging, hard on a marriage. She kept thinking, W-D 40 needed here.

Jen walked past the box men, and studied the full pallets so the men would think she was keeping an eye on them. The women slowed their conversational Spanish when she came around, so that she could keep up with them. The men, on the other hand, talked faster. They had nicknames for everybody. "Chewing Gum" for Nora, the slow packer, "Princess" for Teresa, the haughty packer. She hated to think what their nickname for her was. The boxes were heavy, and it was considered macho work, so the most strapping young men vied for this job, their jeans tight across narrow buttocks, their T-shirt sleeves rolled up over bulging arms, their brown skin gleaming with sweat. They were hard workers, but they chafed at directions from a woman. Sometimes they responded better to Tom's curses and harassments than they did to her. They eyed her sideways from under heavy lashes, and shrugged when she pointed out a box that had been stacked on the wrong pallet, as if these things happen. "*Si, si.*" What could they do? "*No le hace.*" She had invented secret nicknames for them, in silent retaliation:

"Slow Motion," "Macho Man." Sometimes their disdain for her was tauntingly casual. Sometimes their eyes fixed on her hips with irritating sexuality. Sometimes she could feel their animosity strike her as sharply as if they had thrown pebbles at her back. But when she turned to face them, she saw only their lidded eyes looking at her about chest high and their mocking mouths pulled tight.

"Cuidado!" She jumped back out of the way of a careening forklift. She hadn't heard it coming in the din of the machinery. The men laughed. Forklift drivers were modern-day cowboys, indispensable, skilled, reckless. They drove as if they were entered in a barrel race. The driver gave her a dazzling smile and missed her toe by four inches. Forklift drivers all drove a little too fast and cut the corners a little too close. "Look where you're going!" she yelled. He couldn't hear her. Her secret nickname for this guy was "Gunsmoke." God, it was hot.

She retreated to the packing line and put her arm around Maria Ruiz, the head packer. Maria was small and dainty and ageless, with dark curly hair and gold rimmed spectacles. She wore a gentle smile and a freshly-ironed pinafore apron over her shirt and pants. She'd worked at the shed since Jen was a little girl. Jen addressed her as Doña Maria. Maria was too kind to the packers who worked under her, most of whom were related to her, some who took advantage of her. Maria's husband drove tractor on the ranch. Maria had raised five children and sent the oldest boy to the University of California at Davis, working long days every summer at the packing shed. Jen's father said the rest of the Ruiz kids were no good. Jen suspected that Maria's meager resources just hadn't stretched to the other children. There was so little money, so little space, so little energy left over. There stood Maria, smiling, after six hours on a concrete slab that made your shins ache just looking at it.

The pear packers were the aristocracy of the packing shed. Packing was piecework. The packers were paid by the box, rather than the hour, like the rest of the shed workers. Teresa, the best packer made $125-$150 a day. The work was backbreaking, hot, monotonous and required as much dexterity as playing the piano eight hours a day while standing up. Teresa's hands flew from wrapping tissue to pear to box, wrapping tissue, pear, box. The young women packers laughed and teased and kindly encouraged and corrected Jen's Spanish, chatting with her while their fingers moved so quickly Jen couldn't focus on them.

"*Que calor*, Doña Maria," Jen said, noticing that Maria looked fresh, unaffected by the heat, while Jen herself felt her hair caked on her forehead, sweat trickling down her neck and under her arms.

"*Ay, como un horno*," Maria said, like an oven, enunciating her words for Jen, shaking her head sympathetically. Jen sometimes had the feeling that while the young box men despised her, Maria Ruiz pitied her.

A problem arose. The woman at the scale called out that some of the boxes were underweight. Maria and Jen examined them and found that several boxes were short the required number of pears. "Whose are these boxes, Doña Maria," Jen asked in Spanish, raising her voice to be heard above the clamor.

"I will take care of them."

"But whose are they?"

"*Bien*, I will talk to her." Maria repacked the boxes as she spoke, adding the missing fruit, deftly tucking the printed tissues so that the company name showed on the top of each pear. Then she bustled off to her packers, not meeting Jen's eyes.

Jen looked up the packer's number. It was Nora, as she had suspected, a new packer this year, a dumb, heavy, listless girl and a cousin of Maria's husband. She was slow and clumsy and had been a problem ever since they started packing a month ago. Why was it so damned hot?

"*Cajas! Cajas!*" Someone called out for more boxes. The box men had been sitting around on empty pallets while the packers ran out of boxes. Their packing tissues were running low, too. Jen knew better than to yell across the shed at the box men. They'd turn sullen and slow if she yelled at them in front of the whole shed. She walked over and stood watching while they scrambled to catch up. She filled one belt with boxes herself to shame them, then grabbed an armful of tissues for the packers. As she did she glanced over at the elevator and realized that Tom had turned the speed up again while she had been dealing with the box crisis. The sorters wouldn't be able to keep up, and the machinery would overheat.

She did shout at Tom, but he pretended not to hear her over the noise of the machinery. She ran up the ladder to the control panel and turned the speed down herself. Tom had walked to the other end of the scaffold and pretended not to see her.

This was Tom's first year at the shed. He was a short, grizzled man who wore dirty cowboy boots to make himself taller and a shabby, drooping mustache to make himself look more important. His cowboy shirts were thin, faded and unbuttoned to reveal graying chest hair and a gold chain. He smelled of flat beer and stale cigarettes. He looked to Jen like an old Banty rooster who'd never won a fight.

"Do you speak Spanish?" she had asked him when he had applied for the job.

"Don't need to, Little Lady. I keep a Smith and Wesson 45 on the front seat of my car. That's all these Mexicans understand."

"Just don't ever bring it into my shed." Jen voted against hiring him.

"What can I do, Jen?" the shed foreman asked.. "The fruit's ripe. The guy's a good mechanic, and he's worked with this same equipment in the Northwest."

"Can you work for a woman?" the foreman had asked Tom.

"We'll get along jes' fine, me and the Little Lady."

"*Quizás*," said Jen. We'll see.

From her vantage point up on the scaffold walkway Jen could look right down on Nora as she packed. Nora was leaning against a stool while she worked. She looked pale, clammy. She wiped her forehead with the back of her hand and laboriously packed another layer, leaving the tissues flapping. She was oblivious to Jen standing above her, but Maria Ruiz noticed and came over to help Nora, murmuring something to her. Nora looked up vaguely, scarcely focusing on Jen.

This was ridiculous. Maria was protecting her. She was clearly not trying. She couldn't do the work. If she wanted to stamp boxes, she might work out, but she obviously couldn't pack.

It was only 3:30. And up on the scaffold where Jen stood it was 103 degrees. She ought to get rid of that thermometer.

Jen descended to the floor and went over to Maria and Nora. "Doña Maria," Jen said tersely in Spanish, "this does not go. Nora is not able to do this work."

"Jen," Maria said, "the woman is sick. She will be better tomorrow."

"Then she should stay home if she is sick." Jen noticed the other packers watching her. Their eyes were thick with concealed emotion. "She will give it to the others."

"Jen," Maria said sternly, "it is not that kind of sickness. We will talk later."

Jen knew all about the Mexican women's female complaints—cramps, mysterious pains, headaches. "No, Maria, we will talk now. I must give Nora a first warning. Her boxes are not good."

Jen was aware that all the packers had stopped packing. She couldn't hear them stop over the noise of the shed, the machinery, the forklifts, but she knew that behind her all the women on the packing line watched her, their eyes still and hostile. Their good-natured begrudging of her position as boss, theirs as employees, had soured suddenly. Jen turned. She realized that she was used to the men's macho resistance, to Tom's mean tricks, but that she had counted on the women's goodwill. Their gentle courtesy, their kindness had been like a blessing on her. Now they looked at her much the way the men looked at her. Perhaps they always had. Perhaps they had worn masks of civility. Now their masks had fallen away. Jen looked at them, these quiet, courteous women, and felt panic.

Maria Ruiz took pity on her. "*Querida*," she said quietly, (Jen could barely hear her with all the noise in the shed. Maria had not called Jen "*Querida*" since Jen was a little girl.) "Nora has trouble carrying a child. I think she has lost this one." Maria crossed herself. "She feels unwell."

"Maria, when? Why did you not tell me?"

"At lunch time. You were not here. I took care of it."

"Why did you not tell me, Maria?"

Maria looked up at Jen over her gold-rimmed spectacles. She sighed, "I did not know if you would comprehend."

TACO TRUCK

Anita was tall and lean and intelligent, so she was not popular with men. She possessed an Aztec warrior's face, long and sharply chiseled, nearly handsome. She pulled her straight black hair severely off her face and anchored it with heavy plastic combs to the sides of her head. Thick black lashes guarded her dark eyes. In winter she pruned in one of the orchards, her long, strong fingers, numb from the cold, snapping the pruning shears in the tops of the apple trees, weaving the stiff branches back against the trellis to which they were trained. The north wind cut through the two sweatshirts she wore, one on top of the other, and made her eyes sting. In spring she packed asparagus in a drafty old aluminum packing shed with a cement floor that made her legs ache and broken down packing machinery so loud it made her head throb. But during the summer pear season she cooked in a cookhouse at one of the Mexican labor camps. This was her money job. During those sweltering summers as she chopped the mountains of onions and peppers, stirred the huge iron pots moles and beans, nearly dead on her feet from the twelve-hour days, she dreamed of owning a taco truck.

She lived with her mother and her brother and his wife and three children in a rundown house on the back of the Clark ranch. The roof leaked and the septic tank stank, but it was cheap. She skimped by on her other earnings for most of the year, and then, at the end of each pear season, she took her whole paycheck from the cookhouse to the Bank of Alex Breen and deposited it in her savings account. She kept her passbook in her top drawer, and at night after the family had gone to sleep she would quietly take it out and study it.

Some nights, as she looked at the figures jotted on the lines of the book, she became depressed. I will be ninety years old, she thought, before I can earn enough for my own taco truck. Sometimes she dreamed of her gleaming truck parked beside the Pear Blossom Bridge along the Sacramento River. Long lines of people crowded around Anita's Taco Truck to order her famous tacos. The passbook grew dog-eared from handling, but year by year her savings grew. A few more years, she thought, and perhaps I can buy my taco truck, a used truck to be sure, one with an engine that needs work, a few dents perhaps, a taco truck.

Anita's brother worked as a mechanic for the local tractor dealer. Every week she and he scanned the classified section of the Mexican newspaper printed in Stockton.

"Taco trucks are very expensive," her brother said.

"Even the beat-up ones," Anita said.

"Even the ones with blown engines," said her brother.

Still, Anita dreamed.

Anita's mother died suddenly. A pious, iron-willed woman who had never admitted to illness a day in her life, she was felled by a heart attack. Anita found her one morning on the floor of her bedroom clutching her rosary. No one had heard her fall. Many years earlier she had made Anita and her brother swear that they would send her body back to Mexico to be buried beside their father. Anita looked at her mother lying wide-eyed, staring accusingly, and she knew her dream of a taco truck had died with her.

By the time Anita and her brother had paid for the mortuary, the casket, the airfare, the burial, the masses in their hometown of Tecate, Anita's savings had vanished, and her brother was deeply in debt. Now that her mother was gone, her sister-in-law began to openly resent Anita's presence in the house. She began to hint that Anita should pay a larger share of the rent. Anita's brother grew depressed and began to drink too much beer. Anita's dream of a taco truck was dead, finished.

A month later her brother came home with devastating news. "A taco truck has set up shop next to the Pear Blossom Bridge," he said. "It looks like he's there to stay. He has put a card table in front with a table cloth and a pot of flowers," her brother added sourly.

Her place. Beside the river. The place Anita had dreamed of parking her taco truck. Anita crawled into her bed that night clutching her worn out savings pass book and cried herself to sleep.

The next day at lunchtime Anita went to the Pear Blossom Bridge. There, just as Anita had imagined it, stood a gleaming silver taco truck. She felt as if she were dreaming. She parked off the road twenty yards away from the truck and stared. It was *guapo. Ay,* it was *muy guapo.* She couldn't remember ever seeing a handsomer taco truck. A Chevrolet dual-axle truck clad in shiny aluminum siding that was stamped in a diagonal quilted pattern. White fiberglass hatches opened on the roof of the truck to let the fresh river breeze blow through. Two more hatches lifted up on one side to make a generous awning and a little counter. Under the awning a screened window allowed the customers to give their orders and take their food. It was a magnificent truck. Her eyes watered.

Anita got out of her car and approached the beautiful truck. A line had formed at the window, so she had time to study the truck closely. The menu board was painted bright red with yellow lettering. It offered the burritos and tacos favored by the local farmers and fishermen: *asada, pollo, carnitas.* But it also advertised the Mexican delicacies: the *lengua,* the *buche,* and the *cabeza.* For twenty-five cents extra one could order *taco de tripa,* the tripe taco. This was an authentic taco truck. It would be a success here. The workers would flock to this truck, as well as the farmers and fishermen.

She scanned the sign. It was not neatly painted. Anita had excellent penmanship. She could print a better menu board. And the napkin holder and the salsa bottles were not topped up. She surveyed the scene. The tablecloth on the card table was dirty. They should use oilcloth that would wipe off. And real flowers; not plastic ones.

When her turn came to order, Anita could scarcely breathe. Arrayed in the window of the truck were the Jarritos sodas, lime and tamarind and orange, and the hard Mexican candies Anita loved, the round rose covered tins of the De La Rosa peanut butter candies.

"*¿Señora?*"

She realized the man inside the truck was staring at her curiously, waiting for her order. "*Buenos dias, Señor,*" she said politely. You have a beautiful taco truck."

"Thank you, *Señora,*" the man replied. "What may I offer you?"

The man and his wife worked side by side inside the taco truck. The wife scolded the husband in Spanish as she cooked at the stove. Anita gave her order, then stood aside and listened.

"Don't put so much meat in the tacos," the wife scolded. "Not so much cilantro. We will go broke giving so much away."

Anita pretended to be looking at the candies.

"Why do you insist on *tacos de cabeza?*" complained the wife. "As soon as you tell people it is beef head, they order something else. It is a waste. All these people know is chicken and beef."

The husband put Anita's *taco de lengua* on a little paper tray and added a wedge of lime, two crisp slices of radish and a plump pickled *jalapeño* pepper.

"Many thanks," said Anita, and she smiled her most disarming smile. "This smells delicious. You are very generous."

"Too generous," muttered the wife in Spanish. "You give everything away."

It was difficult to see the wife clearly through the screen window, but she appeared to be short, with a broad bottom and fat fingers that gripped her spatula like a club. She had dyed hair the color of kidney beans.

The taco was a good taco, although Anita thought her own *lengua* was much better. Beef tongue must be cooked slowly for a long time or it becomes tough, she thought. Also the seasoning is critical. It must not be bland, but one must be careful not to overwhelm the delicate flavor of the tongue. Still, she complimented the man. "This is a delicious taco, the best I have ever tasted," she said. "From where do you come?"

"Stockton," said the man. "Guadalajara before that. We have just bought this truck."

"It is an excellent taco truck," Anita said. "Do you require help? I am a cook."

"No," the wife broke in. "Can't you see? We are crowded in here as it is."

"Well, thank you and good fortune to you," said Anita politely, and she smiled her sweetest smile at the man.

He smiled at her and bowed courteously. "Thank you. Many thanks."

Every week after that Anita went to the taco truck and ordered a different kind of taco. Every week the man greeted her courteously, and the wife turned her back on her and ignored her. Every week Anita heard the wife haranguing the man in a shrill, piercing voice, like a nail scratching the side of the taco truck "Why do we serve *tripa*. Nobody likes it. We always have to throw some away." or "You burn the beans, and then I have to scrub the pot." Every week Anita pretended not to hear.

Anita complimented the man on his tacos, particularly the *taco de tripa*. "Your beans are especially delicious," she said. Every week she took silent inventory of what was wrong with the truck. The screen across the window needed replacing. There was a hole in it, and flies buzzed against the inside of the window. She grew a great clump of cilantro at her house. It was fresher and more flavorful than the limp cilantro the woman hoarded. The chicken was tough. They needed to cook it more gently. Anita grew and pickled her own *jalapeños*. The pickled vegetables the man served were of inferior quality. She knew a much better brand. She could buy those things at the wholesale house in Stockton along with better napkins and fresher *salsa*. The head cook at the cookhouse had taught her where to buy the best ingredients for the cheapest prices.

And every week she smiled sweetly at the man and complimented him on his delicious tacos and his handsome truck. Anita began to take a little more trouble with her hair. She began to gather it up in a soft coil at the nape of her neck. She bought a new lipstick in a soft coral color, and she wore scooped-neck blouses that showed her round breasts to better advantage.

One day the man was alone. "Your wife is ill?" She asked politely.

"She has had to go back to Mexico. Her mother is sick with the cancer."

"Would you like some help, just for the day? I am not working today. I could wash up those pans for you. You must be tired," she said gently.

The man smiled. "I would like to, but . . ."

"Oh, I would not want payment. It would be enough to work in such a beautiful truck."

"Thank you. If you are sure . . ."

Anita climbed up inside the taco truck, donned a dishtowel and went to work. She scrubbed every pot. She attacked the grease on the burners. The wife had not cleaned the stove properly. She polished the stainless steel counter until it shone; she organized the paper trays and the paper napkins. She filled the salsa bottles. As she worked, she chatted cheerfully with the man as if this were the most fun in the world, playing inside his shiny taco truck.

Miguel was his name, Miguel Tejada. He had always been hunched over, looking out the window of the taco truck. When she stood beside him and he straightened up to look at her, he was taller than she thought and a little older, with a broad chest, black curly hair and a gentle brown face.

She smiled at him and cocked her head to one side. "You have a handsome truck," she said, "and the best tacos. They are generous tacos. The taco truck up the river at the Courtland Bridge serves inferior tacos. Yours are much better," she lied. "Everybody says so."

The next day she was waiting when Miguel pulled up next to the bridge in his taco truck. She wore a becoming apron, a red gingham pinafore apron with ruffled shoulders that had been her mother's. She carried a bouquet of bright zinnias from her garden. "For the table," she said, and stuck them in an empty tomato can. I must take that cloth home tonight and wash it and iron it, she thought, as she arranged the zinnias on the table.

"Do you have children?" she asked politely as she scrubbed and polished the walls and the counters at the end of the lunch rush.

"No," Miguel said. "God has not given us children yet."

Anita's heart leapt for joy. "Let me help you tomorrow. I could do some of the cooking too. You deserve a little rest now and then." She accidentally rubbed against his hip as she bent over to put away a pot. "Now, I will just run to the market for two beers, and we will relax a moment. You must be very tired."

It was as she and Miguel sat at the table with the dirty tablecloth that her brother passed by on his way home from work.

"What do you think you're doing," her brother demanded when she came home an hour later. "All of Pear Blossom saw you there drinking beer with a married man."

"He hired me to help out," Anita lied. "He pays me good money. He's short-handed."

"Where's his wife?" her brother asked.

"Her mother is sick. She has gone back to Mexico."

"Well, be sure he pays you." Her brother belched, "We need the money."

For two weeks Anita worked at the taco truck. Tourists and fishermen were beginning to stop there as well as the workers from the surrounding orchards. The lines grew longer at lunchtime. At the end of the month Anita added $20 to her share of the rent.

"Because I am earning a little extra," she lied to her sister-in-law.

"And what are you doing to earn that money?" asked her sister-in-law, snatching the $20 dollar bill. "Is it dirty money?"

Anita's handsome chin jutted out. Her black eyes flashed. She turned her back on her sister-in-law and her dark, heavy hair swirled across her face. She walked over to her brother slumped on the sofa with all the stuffing coming out of it. She looked down at him.

"I think I have found my taco truck," she said evenly.

"What? Where?"

"The one at the Pear Blossom Bridge."

"Does he want to sell it?" Her brother took another gulp of his beer, tilting his head back not even looking at her. "No matter, you have no money."

"I think he is interested in me." Anita could hear her sister-in-law gasp behind her.

Her brother glanced up at her, "And the wife?" her brother asked.

Anita shrugged, "She has gone back to Mexico. Who knows?"

Her brother laughed bitterly, turned away, reached for another beer. "*Verdad,*" he said. He shrugged and opened his beer, "Anyway, what have you got to lose?"

"*Exactamente,*" said Anita, looking around the room at the filthy sofa and the wired together chairs and the broken lamp and the water-stained walls. She looked at the sullen, resentful face of her brother's wife. *Exactamente,* thought Anita, remembering the dog-eared passbook in her top drawer, empty after so many years of scrimping and saving. "What have I got to lose?"

THE DITCH

The river ran swift and mud brown, lapping up over the riprap on its banks, dead smooth until the trunk of an old tree swirled past, gouged out of the levee by the current. Dan turned off the levee road down into the orchard. The pear trees were all pruned now, rows of crooked trunks, gnarled, knobby joints. They looked aged and sore. The muddy road sucked at the tires of his Jeep Wagoneer. Black delta dirt, peat-rich, bottomless. Four-wheel drive was no help in this muck. He wouldn't be able to drive out to the back of the ranch. He didn't want to risk getting stuck. His son had enough on his hands without having to hook up a tractor to haul his father out of the mud. His son Rob was doing a good job. He'd taken over the ranch two years ago at Dan's insistence. Rob had earned the right to make his own mistakes. You can't have two bosses on one ranch.

Dan only came out to run his dog Soot, an old black lab who was panting in the back of his Jeep now, anxious to be let out so he could snuffle the tules along the full ditches for the stray mallard or sand hill crane. Dan was surprised to see the tules still there. He had always cleaned out that ditch in late fall.

Soot was the best dog Dan had ever had—a good nose, soft mouth. They'd hunted together for years, crouched in a blind to watch the cold, pre-dawn breeze riffle the duck ponds and creep down the back of Dan's neck so that he hunched his shoulders and turned up the collar of his hunting jacket. Soot lay beside him, never moved a muscle. Together they watched for the sun to break the horizon, lighting the ponds turquoise, gilding the rice stubble.

Then the flights of ducks would start to work in, circling high, spiraling down, and Soot's body would tense, waiting for Dan to pick out a swift, low-flying teal or a fat sprig. The sound of Dan's shotgun would send Soot leaping out across the water, splashing in the sunlight, returning wet and happy with the duck held gently in his mouth. Not a mark on it.

Their hunting days were mostly behind them. Dan's cataracts were bad, and Soot's joints had stiffened up. His hind legs betrayed him from time to time. When he chased some bird into a ditch, Dan had a hell of a time hauling him out again. But Soot still loved the ranch. Dan didn't have the heart to deny him a run every day. Dan liked being out there himself, though he didn't want to be seen as interfering.

Actually he timed his morning visits so that his son was usually at Ike's Café for coffee, catching up on the local news, keeping his ear to the ground. Most of the farmers dropped by Ike's about 10:00 in the morning after they'd gotten things going on their ranches. They traded stories about levee breaks and truck mechanics and wheat prices. They caught up on the latest gossip. Dan had stopped going to Ike's when he turned the ranch over to Rob. One Murphy was enough on the stools at Ike's. His generation was mostly gone anyway. The men at Ike's were his son's age now, the generation that left their hats on at the counter, ball caps mostly—Giants caps, camouflage hunting caps, UC Davis caps. Never took 'em off, inside or out. It had driven his wife Ellie crazy.

He always removed his hat when he walked in the door—an old weather-beaten Stetson, a Gunnison, narrow-brimmed, mushroom gray, with a sweat-stained hatband. "Disreputable," Ellie had called it, but she worried about skin cancer so she didn't scold him. She'd shake her head and sigh, "That old thing." But then she'd laugh. Oh, Ellie had such a laugh. It bubbled up inside her, warm as bath water, filled with sunshine. Her whole face lit up when she laughed.

The young men Rob's age favored T-shirts and running shoes in the summer, fleece and Gore-tex boots this time of year. Dan still wore the high bird-shooting boots he ordered from the L.L. Bean catalogue and blue chambray work shirts from the local dry goods store. His housekeeper Mitzuko insisted on starching and ironing them, even though they said NO IRON on the label. Actually, she was Ellie's housekeeper, not his. The two women had run the household for years, a strong sisterhood based on limited English, a lot of Clorox, a passion for dahlias and an aversion to mice. Since Ellie died Mitzuko had gotten bossy. She insisted that he wear a clean white undershirt and a fresh work shirt every day. She stood over him every morning with his blood pressure pills, interrupting his crossword. It was as if she and Ellie had made some sort of a pact. Dan could almost hear Ellie saying, "I don't want him going around looking disheveled." Disheveled. Disreputable. Those were the kind of words Ellie used. He smiled.

Both he and Soot took glucosamine for their joints, too, though he couldn't see that it helped either one of them much. It irritated him that his pills cost more than Soot's. He had complained to Fred at the pharmacy. Fred had looked over his eyeglasses at Dan and said levelly, "Because I need the money more than the vet does." That was Fred for you.

Now Dan had time to do the crossword every morning. In ink. That was a matter of some pride to him.

Meanwhile the men his son's age sat at Ike's Café with their caps on and talked about computer problems and cell phone coverage. Rob knew he ran Soot on the ranch every morning. Dan wasn't sneaky about it. He just didn't want to be in the way.

He drove out as far as he dared, feeling the sliminess of the mud under his wheels, feeling the back end of his wagon fishtail. Out behind the orchard he stopped and let Soot out. Soot ranged along the main drainage ditch, nose to the ground, tail working. A hawk swooped low over the plowed field behind the ditch. It spotted Soot, and Dan watched it flare up, its tail glowing rusty red in the sunshine. The tule fog had burned off early this morning.

Over to the left, white egrets dotted a vivid green alfalfa field. Soot chased after the nearest one, which lifted off the ground and settled unconcerned twenty yards further down the field. Soot, insulted, barked. Dan laughed. "They don't take us seriously any more, Soot. Come on. Back in the Jeep."

Soot understood him but pretended not to, dawdling back along the ditch. A pond turtle dove into the water and disappeared in the muck. Dan saw Soot think about plunging after it, whistled him back, forgetting for the moment that Soot had begun to go a little deaf. The dog disappeared over the side of the ditch and came up paddling around in circles just as Dan reached the edge.

"God damn it, Soot, get out of there."

Soot was trying. He'd given up on the turtle. He tried to scramble up the bank, but it was steep, the tules and cattails were slippery, the mud was slick and the water was too high for him to get a foothold on the bottom of the ditch. He slid down the bank, hind end first, and splashed helplessly. Dan leaned over and called to him, tried to grasp his collar as Soot scratched for a foothold on the side of the ditch, but, just as Dan thought he had him, Soot's gimpy back legs went out from under him, and he slipped back into the water again. He was beginning to tire. His head was lower in the water.

Dan knelt beside the ditch cursing, finally got down on his belly and leaned over the edge, grabbed at Soot, finally got hold of his collar and pulled. Soot clawed at the bank with his front legs, lunging forward, but his back legs dragged uselessly behind him. Dan hauled him part way up the side, but Soot couldn't help much. Dan didn't have the strength to get him out. Soot slid back down. The sides were too damn straight. The ditch was maybe ten feet wide. How deep? Three feet? Four feet?

Dan opened the back of his Jeep, took off his hat and his jacket and his boots. He grabbed a tarp and his irrigating boots. His irrigating boots wouldn't help much. The water was too high. They'd probably just weigh him down, but he was damned if he would ruin a good pair of bird shooting boots. He reached for a rope and tied it to the hitch on the back of his Jeep. He used it to lower himself into the ditch, sliding most of the way on his butt. The water came up to his mid-thighs. By now he was slick with mud. Mitzuko would have a fit. From inside the ditch he could get a hand under Soot's back end and give a good push. Soot revived a little seeing Dan in the ditch with him. He scratched his way up Dan's pant leg and shirt, across his face, leaving a wet-dog smell, and finally, with a heave from Dan, onto the bank, where he stood shivering for a minute. Then he gave himself a good shake and peered over the edge of the ditch at Dan.

"God damn it, Soot," Dan roared, "Sit!"

Soot sat, but he looked worried. Dan surveyed the side of the ditch, trying to catch his breath, looking for a foothold. How the hell was he going to get out? He still held the end of the rope. He'd just have to find some kind of purchase for his foot half way up the side. He realized he was getting cold. He'd better get a move on. Soot looked over the edge at him and barked.

"Quiet, Soot." Christ, he didn't want Soot alerting one of the men on the ranch. That's all Rob needed. To have his crew drop everything to rescue his father from a drainage ditch. But now Soot was getting frantic. He looked over the edge front paw cocked, ears forward, tail quivering. Dan had better get to it or Soot would come in after him, and there they'd both be. He wiped his palms on his shirt and grabbed the rope with both hands. Pulling his foot out of the mud on the bottom of the ditch was harder than he expected. He chose a clump of cattails at water's edge and placed his right boot firmly into the roots. He took a deep breath and pulled himself up, kicking up the slimy stench of dead tules, but his right boot kept slipping on the rotting weeds, and his left foot stayed stuck in the mud. By the time he had worked his left foot out he'd lost his grip and his right foot was caught half way up the side in the cattails. His hands slipped and he fell backwards into the water. Soot barked frantically above him, running back and forth along the ditch.

"Stay!" Dan yelled. The mud on the bottom had sucked off his left boot. He felt around for it with his foot, but it was gone. He was getting seriously cold. He found the rope, wet and slimy now, and heaved himself up as far as a clump of tules. He lay clinging to it and to the rope for a moment to catch his breath, then crawled on his belly pulling on the rope and the tules, slipping back, catching himself, clawing his way up the bank through the dead weeds. He collapsed face down in the mud beside the Jeep. Soot licked his ear.

He had to get up. He'd catch pneumonia lying there in the mud with the cold breeze catching his wet hair, the back of his shirt. He had to get up. If he didn't one of the men from the ranch would discover him lying there and raise an alarm. The thing he resented most about getting old was this loss of strength. He'd gotten so damned weak. Soot nosed his hair, whined. Dan raised his head and looked into the wet, black face of his dog, gray around the muzzle now, a little overweight. Dan suspected Mitzuko of slipping him crusts of buttered toast the way Ellie had. Soot crouched on his haunches as if playing a game of fetch.

"All right, all right." Dan muttered. He got to his knees. The breeze caught him full in the chest and made him cough. Reaching for the hitch on the Jeep, he pulled himself up, waited for his left knee to straighten, take some weight. He untied the rope, took off his remaining irrigating boot, dumped the water out of it. He put Soot, the rope and his boot in the back, pulled off his shirt and climbed into the Jeep shivering. Once he started the engine, got the heater going, he wiped himself down as best he could with his cotton undershirt. Mitzuko had put a box of Kleenex under the seat. He grabbed a handful of tissues and wiped his face, ran his fingers through his hair. He put on his hat, zipped his jacket up to his chin, wrung out his socks and laced up his bird shooting boots. Only his Levi's were wet. He should have taken them off. He leaned against the steering wheel of his Jeep and let the hot air from the heater vent blow against his face.

As Dan drove back through the ranch headquarters he was surprised to see his son Rob's pickup in front of the barn. He'd banked on slipping out unseen. How long had he been in that ditch? It must be later than he thought. Rob waved at him and walked over. Dan lowered the window of his Jeep part way.

"Hi, Dad. Glad to catch you. I wonder if you could take a look at the pump with me. It's acting up again. I hate to call Charlie. He's probably up to his ass in emergencies with the river so high."

All the islands in the Delta depended on their pumps running twenty-four hours a day in the winter to keep the ditches emptied. Otherwise the river seeped in under the levees, flooding the orchards, turning the middle of the islands into lakes. Charlie was the only electrician in the area. He worked eighteen-hour days this time of year.

Dan had thought the ditches looked a little high, though he wouldn't have said anything. He left Soot in the back of his wagon, grabbed his work gloves, pulled his hat a little lower and followed Rob up over the levee and down to the river's edge. Dan fought his way through the pipe weed and dead anise stalks, shivering a little, treading carefully so as not to slip and make a fool of himself. They crouched together around the pump, sweeping the black widows out of the housing with their work gloves. Rob ran a flashlight over the workings, catching his dad's face in the beam.

"You look a little wet," he said.

"Soot got stuck in the ditch again. Had a hell of a time getting him out." He looked at the pump. "So, what's it doing?"

Obviously there was going to be no further explanation of his father's wet hair and soaked, mud-smeared jeans. "It keeps cutting out," Rob said.

The pump was as old as Dan was and as ornery. It looked like the innards of an old Model T had been dumped over the side of the levee and settled here above high water, all leaky valves and blown seals. It had plagued Dan for thirty years, always failing when it was needed most, in the middle of harvest, when the river reached flood stage. Charlie's father had sworn at it for thirty years, too.

Dan avoided his son's eyes, studied the pump. He'd been a genius, Charlie's dad. Everything he'd learned he'd learned in the army during the war, he said. He'd been assigned to keep medical outfits going 24/7: generators, Jeeps, mobile surgery units. He could do more with a bad switch or a hot wire than any man Dan had ever known. He died a painful, lingering death, a cancer that ate away at him. Didn't deserve it. Wasn't anybody on the river he hadn't done a favor for. His son Charlie was a nice guy, but he couldn't hold a candle to his dad when it came to fixing things.

Dan straightened up. Crouching wasn't as easy as it used to be. He was cold and stiff. He waited for the leg cramp to pass. "Smells like it might be overheating," he said.

"Could be."

"Tried a new belt?"

"No, we don't have one in the shed."

Dan had always made it a practice to keep two or three belts in reserve just in case. "Well, it's either that or a new bearing," he said. "Son of a bitch goes through belts. Soot and I could run up to Charlie's shop and see if he's got one."

"That would be great, Dad. I promised I'd meet that new labor contractor here at 11:00. I'd appreciate it if you're not too busy."

"No, Soot's had his run."

He let his son lead back up the levee so Rob wouldn't notice his wet Levi's, wouldn't see him breathing hard or clinging to the pipe weed to pull himself up the bank. Dan got back in his Jeep, and Soot climbed over the seat to sit beside him. He was covered with mud from head to tail.

Rob smiled, "Soot had himself a good time. Did he catch anything?"

"Just a bunch of pond weed."

Rob laughed and waved.

Dan closed the window and turned the heater fan up to high. Soot liked riding shotgun and Dan liked the company. Since Ellie died he talked to Soot a good deal. And he had a few things to say to him now.

Rob stood in the yard and watched the two heads disappear around the corner of the barn, Dan and Soot, side by side, in the front seat of his dad's Jeep. He wondered what kind of trouble they had gotten themselves into out there in that ditch. They were both soaked to the skin. His dad looked exhausted, a little shaky. He wondered how bad his dad's cataracts were, whether he ought to be driving.

Dan drove out the ranch gate, up onto the levee road. He unzipped his jacket and let the heater warm his bare chest. He coughed. "Soot," he said, "you son of a bitch, we pulled it off this time, but I haven't got many more of your swimming parties left in me." He scratched Soot behind his left ear, and Soot rubbed his head against Dan's hand. "Mitzuko's gonna give us both hell, you know that."

POT FARM

It was Elsie at the Post Office got wind of it first. Elsie mentioned it to Dennis Reilly when he came in for his mail and Margaret Lyon's mail too. Margaret was a widow who lived next door and ought not to be driving. Whenever people in town saw Margaret hunched at the wheel of her '83 Cadillac, peering up over the dashboard like a dormouse, they were careful to keep their distance.

When Dennis went in for coffee at Ike's Café that morning he asked the deputy sheriff if he knew anything about it. Dennis was careful to keep his voice down. These sorts of rumors spread like chickenpox on the river. But Ike was refilling saltshakers at their end of the counter, so he happened to pick up a few words.

Scott, the deputy sheriff, looked at Dennis as if he hadn't heard him right. It had been a bad week for Scott. Old Man Baroni had been at it again with his wife, and this time she'd called the sheriff's office, loaded her husband's shotgun and dared Baroni to step one foot inside the house. The Dwyers were evicting a migrant family from a run-down house on Third Street, and that too had resulted in a fistfight and a broken nose. Plus, Scott's daughter was kicked off the softball team just before the championship because of a bad grade in algebra.

"What do you mean a marijuana farm?" Scott asked a shade too loudly. The counter at Ike's Café went suddenly silent. Dennis explained that Elsie at the Post Office had noticed a lot of official-looking letters being sent to a certain P.O. Box number. They were addressed to Delta Diversified Farming, which was new to her. But it was the return addresses that caught her eye: Cannabis Policy Project, Alternative Health Centers, Canna Solutions.

Scott sighed. "Great," he said. "Next we'll have the Mafia trying to shake down the taco trucks."

"Say, don't go sticking your nose into this all by yourself," said Dennis. "It might be dangerous."

"I'm the only sheriff's deputy for twenty miles," groaned Scott. "Who am I gonna call in? The Volunteer Fire Department? Hell, I'm on the Volunteer Fire Department."

The men at the counter chewed over that one for a minute.

"Listen," said Don Hutchinson, "when you find out where this Delta Diversified outfit is, why don't you take some of us along with you to check it out?"

"Oh Christ," said Joe Giannini, "I think I know where it is. I've been watching some greenhouses go up way out on the backside of Andrus Island. It's Bill Barnes's place. I figured he was trying some new half-assed scheme. Remember his hydroponic tomatoes and his alfalfa sprout deal?"

"Holy Cow!" said Don. "I saw him the other day driving a brand new Chevy Silverado. I wondered where he'd . . . ."

"Now, wait a minute," interrupted Scott. "This is all just talk. There may be nothing to it. Let's keep this to ourselves until I have a chance to check this out."

"Let us know then," said Ike, handing him a glazed. "And don't do anything stupid."

"Thanks, Ike," said Scott. He'd sworn off glazed doughnuts, but today he seemed to need one. "And I'm serious. Let's keep this to ourselves."

When Scott walked into the Post Office, Elsie was helping Lois Cummings mail a package to her granddaughter in San Luis Obispo. Elsie gathered up the crumpled wrapping paper, taped it neatly, stamped it. Scott waited until Lois was out the door. "Elsie, this Delta Diversified deal you told Dennis about. Who picks up the mail?"

"Well, that's what's weird, Scott. Different guys. Nobody I know. They all have the key to the P.O. Box, so it's perfectly legal."

This alarmed Scott. Elsie knew everybody in town. She'd been Postmistress forever. She even knew the R.F.D.s. "What time do they come in?"

"About 10:00, I think. I'm usually busy then, so I don't always see them."

"Would you mind giving me a call on my cell phone if you do see them?"

"Sure, Scott, but don't do anything rash. They might be criminals."

"Thanks, Elsie," Scott said and smiled to himself. Imagine a deputy sheriff stumbling across a real criminal.

Scott took to doing his paper work in his car outside the Post Office every day at 10:00 o'clock, and three days later Elsie called.

"He's here," Elsie said breathlessly. "He has a registered letter. Do you want me to stall him?"

"No Elsie. That's fine. I'm right outside."

"Oh, Scott, be careful. He's got mean, squinty eyes."

"I will Elsie. Thanks."

Bonnie Edwards and Mary Anne Squaglia walked out of the Post Office and Don Miller came out lugging a heavy package. Then a slender man Scott didn't recognize walked out and got into a new Chevy truck. Dark hair, mid-thirties, slight limp. Scott let two cars pull out, then followed at some distance.

But Scott figured Joe was probably right. They were headed for the backside of Andrus Island. This had something to do with Bill Barnes. It was just nutty enough. Scott had gone to high school with Bill, and Billy had less common sense than anybody he'd ever known. The other thing about Bill was that he always got caught. When they'd hung the varsity girls' bras and undies from the rafters in the high school gym, they would have gotten away with it except that Bill left his jacket with his wallet in the pocket in the bleachers. When they had gone out drinking in the back sloughs, Billy's outboard had run out of gas on the way home. Scott sighed. This had all the earmarks of a Bill Barnes project.

He dropped by Billy's house that afternoon. Bill was out front fixing a gate. He was using screws that were too short.

"Howdy, Scott," Bill said. "Longtime . . ."

"How you been?" Scott asked.

"Good, real good. You know, I've got me a project that's promising to make serious money."

"That so," said Scott.

"Yeah, it's this medical marijuana farm," said Bill. "All perfectly legal. They're some guys from the Bay Area, real businessmen, well funded. They're paying me $1,000 a month rent on my land and another $1,000 a month to oversee the construction of the greenhouses and the planting. Then they'll pay me to grow the pot and harvest it. They've got these workers who really know what they're doing. You ought to come out, Scott. It's a first-class operation."

"I'd like to," said Scott. "You say it's all legal?"

"Oh, yeah," said Bill. "The county gave them a permit. The county attorney who got it through said these guys paid him $500 an hour to handle the details. First class, I tell you."

"I got time right now," said Scott, "if you're not too busy. I'd like to see it."

Bill abandoned his gate, leaving his tools in the middle of the path. "Sure, why don't you ride with me?" he said. "Delta Diversified leased this Chevy Silverado for me. It's a beaut."

The men drove up onto the levee and around to the back of the island, passing the fireworks stand that had been Bill's last business venture. Bill found that it was just over the county line into a county that allowed fireworks sales. He figured every kid for miles around would come for Fourth of July supplies. Unfortunately, last year had been a bad fire year, and fireworks had been banned in the surrounding four counties.

"Plan to open the fireworks stand this year?" asked Scott.

"Oh yeah. This year should be real good. Late rain. I'll open up two weeks before the Fourth. I've got a two-year supply because of that damned ban last year. Everything's ready to go. And this year they came out with these super-sized Whistling Petes that'll knock your head off. And this new thing called an Astro Rocket. I ordered a case of those."

Bill proudly toured Scott through the greenhouses—raised beds drip-irrigated, drip-fertilized. He showed Scott the filtration system and the adjustable panels to control temperature. The little plants looked real healthy. Bill kicked a pallet of high phosphate fertilizer bags. "That was my idea," he said proudly. "We goose 'em with this stuff, those little suckers will grow six inches a week."

"Only thing is, I'm a little worried about the legal side of it," said Scott. "The federal law is still pretty clear."

"Yeah, but these guys say the state law allows it, and believe me they're doing everything by the book. One of 'em has an M.B.A.," said Bill.

"That so?" said Scott. "Just be sure you get your money up front," said Scott. "And don't sign anything."

But Bill was talking about the perimeter fence, which was heavy gauge, 8-foot cyclone and double padlocked. "You don't have to worry about the local kids, Scott. This stuff is 100% pure, for medicinal use only."

"Keeping this to ourselves" to the men at Ike's Café meant telling only their wives about it and asking if they'd heard anything. And so Emma Pratt, the town beautician, heard about it. And Lou Dell, the waitress at Ike's, asked her boyfriend Kenny, who owned the gas station. In that way by dinnertime the first day most of the town of Pear Blossom was alerted to a potential crime wave of unimaginable proportions and the possible takeover of the town by a drug cartel. No one bothered to ask himself why a drug cartel would want a farming community of 723 souls scattered across a half dozen flood-prone islands in the Sacramento Delta. The threat was there.

Scott spent the next week fending off suggestions from the men at Ike's Café. He ought to call the F.B.I. He ought to form a posse. He'd reported it to the county sheriff's office, but there had been a murder/suicide in Elk Grove, and a deputy had been badly wounded. He figured it would be a while. The traffic on the back levee of Andrus Island increased as men drove by to check out the greenhouses for themselves. They took to carrying shotguns on the gun rack in the cabs of their pickups.

Right off parents began to monitor their teenage children more closely, to impose unreasonable curfews. Mothers wouldn't let their children walk home from the grammar school.

Fortunately the men began to get busy. They had corn and tomatoes to plant, winter wheat to harvest. Pear season was just a couple of weeks away. Their wives were a different story. His own wife Rusty was irate. Rusty was a redhead, and he loved her. But she was prone to irate. She vacillated between irate and hysterical. She also laughed a lot, which made up for the tirades. But at the moment she was stuck in irate.

"Why aren't you doing something?" Rusty ranted. "You have a teen-age daughter. Don't you even care about her? My phone hasn't stopped ringing since this whole thing started."

Finally the newspapers got wind of it, as Scott knew they would. Reporters from Sacramento arrived with TV trucks, cameramen. They wanted him to comment on the "ongoing investigation." Their little town made the headlines: POT FARM CAUSES FUROR; NEW CASH CROP IN DELTA. Then the San Francisco papers picked up the story and reported that the Attorney General was looking into it. Reporters got lost and wandered around the islands filming gyp corn and getting stuck in the mud.

Business was brisk at Ike's Café. Reporters were looking for anybody who would talk. Fortunately, farmers are a reticent bunch. They distrust city folk and don't think it's anybody else's damned business. The minute a stranger appeared at Ike's, they clammed up and waited him out.

Elsie at the Post Office became officious as hell when they tried to grill her. She straightened up to her full height of 5'2", stuck out the chest of her well-pressed postal uniform and spouted Post Office regulations, the privacy of first class mail, freedom of information. You name it. They'd met their match with Elsie.

Luckily, none of the newsmen ran into Billy. He was busy out at his fireworks stand getting ready for the Fourth of July rush.

Meanwhile the marijuana plants were growing like weeds. "This thing is getting out of hand," groaned Scott one night about two weeks later. He had a corn on his little toe that was killing him. He eased his boot off, then his sock, and sat on the edge of their bed examining it.

Rusty came over and sat beside him in her pink nightie. "Scott, honey, the whole town's blaming you for not putting a stop to it. Can't you do something?"

"What am I supposed to do?" asked Scott. "The county has issued permits. The laws are screwed up beyond belief. The sheriff's office isn't even bothering to return my phone calls . . . . Oh, God, now what?"

The siren summoning the Volunteer Fire Department had sounded. This time of night it usually meant a drunk driver had gone off the road into the river. Or else he'd gone off the road into a cornfield, which was better. Scott sighed and replaced his sock and his boot.

"Do you have to go tonight? You're so tired." Rusty loved her husband fiercely, worried about him.

"Of course I have to go, Rusty. I'm a volunteer fireman. I'm on call tonight." Scott kissed her nose, picked up his car keys and headed out into the night.

It was a car accident. George Phillips had fallen asleep coming home from a Kiwanis meeting in Rio Vista. He'd gone off the road and hit a power pole. He was O.K., just bruised from his airbag, but the power pole had crashed down next to Bill Barnes's fireworks stand and started a grass fire.

By the time the Volunteer Fire Department got there poor old George was standing in the middle of what looked like a bad war movie. Sprays of red and gold stars were exploding over his head, crate after crate of firecrackers were bursting like bombs, Whistling Petes shrieked off at crazy angles, and what Scott took to be the new Astro Rockets shot off into the wheat field behind him. Roman Candles lit up the night sky.

George was looking pretty dazed. When they got him to safety and doused the end of the fireworks display they realized that the soaring rockets had set fire to a wheat field 100 yards away. They got back on the fire truck and headed out toward the wheat field, feeling their way along a tractor rut in the thick smoke. A wind was whipping the fire in an easterly direction. It was clear to most of them, even in the dark, that the wheat field was a lost cause. Then another explosion and a burst of flame shot up behind the wheat field, and Scott realized exactly where they were on Andrus Island. A queer expression spread across his face.

He turned to Craig Morgan, the fire chief. "You know what that is," he said quietly to Craig.

Craig slammed on the brakes of the fire truck. "Is it those damned pot . . . ."

"Yeah," said Scott. "And they're double padlocked so we can't get in there, and Bill has got a pallet of high phosphate fertilizer sitting right beside them."

"The hell you say," said Craig admiring the blaze.

"I'm afraid it's going to be a total loss," said Scott grinning.

The men sat in the fire truck and watched the fire roar.

"Hey, Scott," said Craig finally, "does this smoke smell funny to you?"

NO TRESPASSING

NO TRESPASSING. Locals didn't waste words. No polite remonstrance: PLEASE RESPECT PRIVATE PROPERTY. A big hand-lettered sign as you came over the bridge onto the island: NO TRESPASSING. That pretty much covered it.

Not that Jen was trespassing exactly. She'd been coming onto this island since she was a child to see the sandhill cranes. It marked the beginning of winter when the sandhill cranes arrived on their yearly odyssey from arctic lands. They sailed over Dead Horse Island in long wavering bands day after day. Cackling, complaining, they settled into the corn stubble and began their fluttering quadrilles decked out in lipstick red headdresses and ruffled petticoats.

Her father had brought her out to see the cranes as a child, telling her about their exotic journey, where they flew in the spring, wonderful names: Slave Lake, Yellowknife, Saskatchewan. Her eyes would water as she stared out at the delicate gray birds as tall as she was. "Imagine," her father would say, "Fifteen hundred miles, and every year they find their way back to the Sacramento Valley, to the same corner of the same field." He'd taught her the other birds too, the mud hens and the spoonbills and the teal. Someday Jen could hunt with him, he said, but first she had to learn to recognize the ducks in flight: the pale, upstretched underwings and the dark heads of the mallard, the white wing patches of the widgeon, the fast, low, twisting flight of the little teal. Can you be a trespasser on your own childhood?

Still, she was careful to drive slowly, to stay on the ranch roads. The ranch had changed hands. She didn't know who managed it now. Would they even know her family name? She didn't want to attract attention. She dreaded getting stuck in the notorious Delta mud, having to ask for help. Jen was aware that she no longer looked local. Boots in the Delta meant Red Wing, not high-heeled Ferragamos. Locals didn't drive Audis.

It began seven years ago when she fled the Delta after her messy divorce and found a job in San Francisco. There'd been a rift between Jen and her mother at the time. Her mother hadn't approved of her first lover, and she'd said so. Jen remembered the afternoon vividly. Standing in this same kitchen, her mother's back to her, hands busy peeling potatoes at the sink. Jen's new love had gone outside to admire the roses.

"I don't like him, Jennifer."

Jen was stunned. Her warm, loving mother. The one she'd always turned to to kiss her bruised knee when her horse brushed her off on a low hanging limb. It was her father who applied the Mercurochrome and the Band-Aid. "You just disapprove of divorce," she'd said. "You wouldn't like any man I brought home who wasn't David."

Her mother had turned then, the front of her apron dusted with flour, "Your father doesn't like him either. He's manipulative, Jennifer. I don't trust him."

"You don't even know him," Jen had cried and slammed the screen door on her way out. She and her lover had left before dinner. Jen had been even more resentful when her mother turned out to be right. They'd never really mended that fence. From then on she had visited her parents alone. Her mother had never met Alex. Jen had been careful about that. Now she regretted it.

When her mother was diagnosed with cancer Jen had tried to come back as often as she could to give her dad and Mitzuko a break. All that winter she and her mom had come out often to see the sandhill cranes, sitting in her mother's old Ford station wagon, a car everybody in town recognized, knew to steer clear of. Her mother's sight was failing. Sometimes they would bring chicken sandwiches and a thermos of coffee. Her mother could no longer use her binoculars. "They don't do me any good," she'd say, "I just like to hear them chatting." It was a period in their lives when a lot of things remained unsaid between them, but it was a companionable silence. They would sit in the fading sunlight and listen to the birds.

The town kept an eye on her parents, the way small towns do. The volunteer fire chief came by with a list of the home phone numbers of five or six firemen in case they ever needed help. The neighbor brought their garbage can to the end of the drive each week. Men dropped by with a lug of pears or tomatoes, grown men her mother had taught in Sunday School years ago, who still called her Mrs. Murphy out of habit and stood up straight when they came to the door. Her younger brother Rob and his wife lived nearby.

Her mother died slowly, painfully. Pain and medication swamped her sunny disposition, her infectious laugh. She grew thinner, grayer, crankier. Her agony exhausted Mitzuko and her father. Three years after her mother's death her father died quickly, quietly of a heart attack while at the top of a ladder pruning the wisteria. Jen couldn't decide which was more wrenching.

Jen had spent the morning at the house. She'd opened the screen door, surprised that the squeak of it should still sound so familiar, a sound from her childhood along with the satisfying slam as she raced down the steps, her mother's voice yelling after her, "Don't, DO NOT slam that door, Jennifer Alice." With her shoulder she'd held open the screen and addressed the back door with a key. It had never been locked that she could remember. In fact, the lock was stubborn, stiff. She'd had to pull on the door and jiggle the key to get it to turn. Only since her father died had the house been locked up and left under a tangle of climbing roses and gangly wisteria, settling even further, it seemed, into the rich peat dirt of the Sacramento Delta.

It was a white frame farmhouse, two-story, four-square, solid, with a wisp of gingerbread on the eaves to indicate optimism and turned posts holding up the front porch to suggest munificence. Farming had provided a decent living in her parents' day, a life of hopeful springs, backbreaking summers and golden autumns, time for fishing and duck hunting and raising children.

The real estate woman had said the house only wanted "perking up." It did look as if it had dozed off while the family wasn't looking, after her father's sudden death, while her brother struggled with his new law practice, and she broke into journalism in San

Francisco. Their younger brother Rob ran the orchards now, but he was up to his ears in debt and labor problems. Maybe the turmoil of it all had fatigued the old house, accustomed as it was to the seasonal, orderly succession of events in a farming life.

They were lucky, the real estate woman said, to be within commuting distance of Sacramento. These "old gems" along the river were in demand. "Old Gems," she called them, not farmhouses. Wealthy lobbyists were "snapping them up," she said, restoring them to a grandeur most of them had never had, building swimming pools and tennis courts and boat docks.

There was less and less farming left. Most of the orchards along the river had been yanked out. The sons of farmers had moved to Sacramento and San Francisco, trying their hands at insurance or finance. Farming didn't pay. Her brother Jim was an attorney in Palo Alto. She had gone to work for a newspaper in San Francisco. Uncle Buck's orchard had been sold to some real estate developer. Only their family's orchard remained and their parents' house with an acre of land around it and an ancient pear tree in the front yard.

Most of the house had been cleared out. Jen and her brothers had met two weeks before and sorted out the silver and the furniture. The piano would go to the Community Church. The clothes and books went to the Church bazaar. Their mother had boxed up all their mementos long ago—Girl Scout merit badges, her brother's 4-H club ribbons. They'd found the boxes taped and labeled in the attic. They'd had a good time, actually. Afterwards, they had sat at the kitchen table and toasted their parents with the last of their father's bourbon, poured into jelly jars.

"Will you miss it?" Rob asked.

Jim and Jen both knew that once this house was sold their ties to the river would be severed. Rob was still hanging on, but their aunts and uncles were all gone, their cousins scattered. Their childhood spent galloping their crowbait horses bareback through alfalfa fields, rowing homemade rafts in the back sloughs, raising chickens (that had been Jim's terrible idea) all of it would be gone. They could return as tourists. They couldn't call it home.

Jen couldn't imagine how that would feel. All her life the river had been her home. When she drove up from San Francisco she still looked forward to crossing the Antioch Bridge onto the first island of the Delta, driving up onto the first levee lined with wild anise and yellow mustard, to see the river mirroring the sky, not a ripple in the tules. She would always say, "It's so beautiful," and Alex would laugh and say, "You always say that." But it was her world, that flat expanse of tangled waterways stitching together a ripe quilt of wheat fields and tomato fields and orchards under a wide blue sky. She knew something would be missing when she couldn't call it home.

"It's such a part of us," Jen said to her brothers.

"You could buy it, you know."

Alex had said the same thing.

"But there's nobody left now. I'd still be a stranger, divorced. A double outsider. I can't help thinking it's a world about to disappear. The levees are crumbling. Southern California wants all the water."

Jim smiled sadly, "I know. If it weren't for the damned smelt, the water would be gone already, filling swimming pools in Southern California." He raised his jelly jar. "Here's to a world about to disappear."

"I like Alex," Rob said to change the subject. Damn it all, he still lived here.

"Thanks, Robbie. I wish Mom had met him."

"She would have loved anybody who loved you," Jim said.

Jen looked into her jelly jar. "I never introduced him to Mom. It didn't seem worth it."

Jim smiled. "I think Alex could have handled it."

"Yeah, but could Mom?"

"Hell, Dad came around," Rob said. Then he grinned. "Of course he was a Giants fan. That gave him an edge." He raised his jelly jar. "No more eulogies, please. We've had enough of that. The Delta isn't dead yet."

Only the kitchen remained. Jen had volunteered to clear it out herself. She wasn't sure why. The kitchen was as she remembered it, only faded a little, as if over the years her mother and Mitzuko had scrubbed away the shine of the butter yellow paint, the gloss of the cupboards, as if Jen were seeing the kitchen through a thin tissue of memory and time. She had promised the realtor that they would be out by the first. But she lingered at what had been her old place at the kitchen table on a chair that still wobbled slightly. That too felt familiar.

It was in this pale yellow kitchen that she had expected to feel her mother's presence most. There wasn't much—a wooden file box filled with dog-eared 5" x 7" index cards, some nearly illegible where the buttermilk spilled or the chocolate dribbled. Beside the stove there was a chipped stoneware crock that held her mother's whisks and wooden spoons. Beside the sink sat a much mended soap dish that Jen had brought to her from France twenty years ago.

She'd thought there would be more of her mother here. A worn place in the linoleum in front of the sink, perhaps, where her mother had spent so many hours washing the beets and sweet radishes she grew in her vegetable garden, dicing onions, tearing the tender lettuces with soft, pale leaves that had to be picked at the last minute and tasted slightly bitter. Perhaps a path beaten to the stove, where she stirred her sour cherry jam or, in the fall, her applesauce, the most perfect breakfast in the world, those green apples poached in simple syrup and eaten with her mother's toasted sour loaf. Jen must remember to find the recipe for sour loaf, though her bread never tasted as good as her mother's, and who had time to bake bread?

Here in the kitchen, where her mother's presence should be felt the most, there seemed so little left of her. The surfaces were too hard, too impervious: enamel, tile, linoleum. No indentations in the counter tops where the palms of her mother's soft hands had kneaded the dough. Only the cutting board carried scars. Her dad had always kept the knives razor sharp.

After she'd finished up at the house, she had come out to see the sandhill cranes. She had volunteered to write an article for the Nature Conservancy. They had recently bought the island where the cranes wintered, and they wanted to publicize it. She pulled off onto a side berm that looked firm enough, got out her notebook and her bird glasses, but she just sat there enjoying the mild winter afternoon, the mud hens dabbling in the flooded corn stubble. A red tail hawk surveyed the scene too from the next power pole.

She could write the article with her eyes closed, but she loved it out here, even now in winter when the fields flooded and the trees were bare. She rolled down her windows and looked east so the sinking sun illuminated the ponds, played on the white plumage of the tundra swans. She adjusted her bird glasses.

"You stuck?"

She jumped. She hadn't heard him come up behind her. He leaned into her passenger side window. A furrowed, wind-chapped face, crumpled, mud-splattered Stetson, blood-shot blue eyes. She recognized him instantly. "Ted! I didn't know you were still here."

Ted chuckled. "Oh yeah. They'll have to cart me off feet first, I imagine. You're the Murphy girl."

Jen smiled. At forty not many people referred to her as a girl. Not many people could have gotten away with it. Ted Stutz was one of her father's oldest friends, a hunting buddy. He'd managed this ranch as long as Jen could remember. Ted could name every bird on the island, tell you when the cranes would come, which corner of which field they would land in. She climbed out of the car and shook his callused hand. "Jennifer, Ted. Good to see you." She turned and looked out at the flocks of birds. "I love it out here."

Ted turned too. "Never gets old, does it." He laughed. "Not like me."

"Like all of us," Jen said. I just finished clearing out Mom and Dad's house today. It feels sad. Towards the end Mom and I used to come out here a lot. I loved my Mom. I just didn't get to know her very well."

"Well, she wasn't easy to get to the bottom of."

"Then we weren't on such good terms toward the end."

"I don't know. She was crazy about you, I know that. And your dad was so proud of you."

"He never said so. It was always, '98%. Why not 100%? Why not an A+?'"

Ted laughed, "Then he'd come and brag about you. I'll tell you when you were accepted to Stanford, the whole town was sick to death of hearing about it."

"Once the house goes, we won't have any ties left to the river. Rob's still here, but Jim and I will be outsiders. Then there's my divorce. This isn't the most liberal place in the universe."

Ted looked at her, studied her for a minute. "No," he said.

"I told the Nature Conservancy people I'd write an article for them. About this island, the cranes. I felt like I was trespassing today, coming out here."

Ted leaned over stiffly, scooped up a handful of black dirt. "Jenny Murphy, don't you remember what your dad always said about this peat dirt? 'The best dirt in the world,' he called it."

Tears came to Jen's eyes. She nodded.

"You think it's not in your blood, this dirt? It don't have anything to do with houses or who you're living with. It's the dirt."

They stood together looking out at the flooded fields. A pair of mallards glided by, leaving a gentle wake in the still water. A flock of mud hens waddled up onto the bank.

"Ted, would you read my piece before I send it in? I don't want to write anything dumb."

"Hell, Jenny, you won't write anything dumb. It's part of you." He patted her on the back. "Don't get stuck."

MEAN DOGS

The heavy black sedan gunned down the ranch road, muscling over ruts, raising dust, inciting the ranch dogs to chase after it, barking and snapping at its chrome wheels. The dogs were a rangy mongrel trio, inbred, wall-eyed, mean. They ran with their yellow tails turned up and their noses high. When the car pulled up in front of the barn, the dogs ganged up on the driver's side snarling.

Rob stood in front of the barn and watched the two men in the automobile sit for a moment, hesitating to open their doors. It occurred to him that he could just leave them there. Maybe they would go away if he just waited. But he knew they wouldn't go away. They smelled a kill. He stepped forward, and the dogs, cowards all three, slunk off to the woodpile beside the barn.

The two men were wearing casual dress. Rob guessed that was what it was—collared polo shirts with insignias from some famous golf course, pressed dark jeans, polished loafers. Their dark glasses looked expensive. They were both tanned in a smooth even tone, probably a result of lying on a beach somewhere. Rob had a "farmer's tan" up to the elbows, the back of his neck, his nose, his ears and a bald spot on the top of his head burnt dark red. He'd been up since 4:30 this morning, getting the pickers going, and he was tired and hungry. For once he had some sympathy with the dogs.

He ushered the men into his office in the front corner of the barn, partitioned off from the tractors and the ranch equipment by a couple of pieces of wallboard thrown up thirty years ago. No ceiling; the pigeons came and went. A dented file cabinet and an old safe crowded against the back wall. A desk and two dusty desk chairs filled the space. His wife had tried to paint the walls once, yellow, but now they were water stained and mud splattered. A Noah Adams lumberyard calendar, two years old, provided the only décor.

The men were developers. They needed "mitigation land." They had already bought the Giannini ranch next door. They used the "conservation credits" to weasel county permits for high-density housing developments closer to Sacramento. They had offered him a price for the ranch that he couldn't refuse. He knew it, and they knew it. They'd done their homework. They seemed to know better than he did how much he owed on the ranch, how much he had lost on the pear crop last year and the year before. He guessed his complete financial statement was probably tucked in that saddle leather briefcase the younger man carried. They had come to close the deal.

"Have you driven around the ranch yet?" he asked. "You ought to know what you're buying."

"No, but we have the county maps," the younger man said.

"Yeah, but have you <u>seen</u> it?" Rob asked.

"We're on a fairly tight schedule," the older man said. Peyton was his name, Peyton Reynolds . . . or was it Reynolds Peyton? Rob couldn't remember.

"It won't take long," he said, grabbing his keys. "You'd better come with me. That car of yours doesn't have much clearance." He walked out of his office to his truck. Peyton! Did this guy grow up being called Peyton? Was there a nickname for Peyton? No wonder the man was such an ass. He climbed in his SUV and waited. They didn't want to see the ranch. He knew that. It wasn't a ranch to them at all. It was "mitigation credits," whatever the hell that meant. Why was he insisting they see the land? He had a mean streak in him, he decided, like those damn ranch dogs. He waited.

In a minute the men emerged from his office, looking over their shoulders for the dogs, and climbed into his SUV, the younger one still clutching the briefcase. The dust inside his Ford was as thick as the dust on the outside. The front seat was littered with coke cans and key rings and pump fittings. He kept his tools in a lug box in the back, but washers and pear rings and sprinkler heads and grease rags covered the back seat. He swept them onto the floor.

"One of you can sit in front," he said.

The younger man climbed in the back, brushing the seat before he sat down. Peyton got in front. They won't be as clean when they make their next call, thought Rob. He drove slowly out into the orchard, down the avenues that smelled of fallen, fermenting fruit. The trees looked dusty, exhausted this time of year. The harvest was nearly over, and the first rains hadn't rinsed away the grime of the season. The leaves had faded but not fallen. Stray branches shot up and out akimbo. In another month or two, after the trees had shed their leaves, they would be pruned into neat rows again, but now they looked straggly, unkempt. He drove "dead slow," he explained, to keep the dust down. "It's bad for the trees," he said. It wasn't great for the pressed dark jeans either, he thought. Reynolds was beginning to sweat and trying to brush off his pants.

He took them to the back of the property, to the main canal that ran along the back of the ranch, bordered now with golden cattails and deep red curly dock. A pair of mallards glided on its green surface. A turtle plopped off the bank and disappeared. He had hunted frogs in this canal because his mom told him French people ate frogs. But when he turned up at the back door with a gunnysack full of frogs she had refused to cook them. "You're going to have to go to France if you want to eat frogs, Robbie," she'd said. "Put them back in the ditch where they belong." He'd like to go to France someday. He'd promised his wife Katy they would after he sold the ranch. She had a poster of some picnic on a river tacked up on the kitchen wall. By Renoir, she said. She wanted to see that river. She wanted to see Paris. Notre Dame, The Eiffel . . . .

The young man in the back seat interrupted his daydream. "What are those guys doing lying around in the orchard this time of day?"

"Eating their lunch," Rob said.

"At 10:30 in the morning?" the young man scoffed.

"They've been up since 4:30, picking by first light," Rob said. "They don't keep bankers' hours." These guys knew nothing about pear growing. How could they possibly run an orchard when their first appointment in the morning couldn't be before 10:00? But, of course, they didn't want to run a pear orchard. They wanted "mitigation land."

He drove past the cornfield that was being disked up and pointed out the hawks that followed the tractor looking for rodents, swooping down as the dark dirt clods turned over. Red tails, northern harriers. Ahead of them a cock pheasant, flushed out of the stubble by the approaching tractor, sailed low over the road into the next field.

He and his older brother Jim had hunted that field as kids, plodding through the corn stubble after their dad's hunting dog, Red, arguing over whose turn it was to carry the gun. Their dad gave them one shotgun between the two of them, an old twenty gauge. "That way you can't shoot each other simultaneously," he said. "And if I ever catch you pointing it at anything other than a cock pheasant you won't have a gun at all." When Dad laid down the law, there was no argument. He meant it.

So Red would point at a pheasant, the dog quivering all over with excitement as she froze that bird in the stubble. The brother without the gun would kick up the bird and yell "hen" if it was a hen. If it was a cock the other boy would take aim, leading it a little as it gained height, and fire. Then they'd trade. Nine times out of ten they missed. Red would turn and look at them disgusted. They spent a lot of mornings in that cornfield, a red sun rising up through the river mist, dew tracing the spider webs silver. They eventually learned to hunt. Jim was gone now. Heart attack last year at forty-five.

Peyton said it looked like pretty good soil.

"Good?" Rob said, "Christ, the topsoil on this island is twenty feet deep. You couldn't find better land."

The younger man was getting antsy in the back seat, fiddling with his brief case. They reached the west end of the ranch.

"This is the beginning of the ranch you just bought," he said, "the Giannini place." He stopped the truck and looked out. "What are you going to do with it?" he asked.

"Well, the trees will have to go," the young man piped up from the back seat. "Too high maintenance."

Rob looked in his rear view mirror at the young man's face.

"We'll just turn it into grazing land or something," the young man continued.

Rob looked out at Giannini's orchard. Giannini was a good grower. The trees were old but well cared for. The centers had been kept open to let sunlight in. They had been carefully pruned and kept free of blight. Rob turned back toward the ranch headquarters.

There was a company operating in the Delta now, a tree removal company. They came in with heavy equipment and yanked the trees out of the ground and left them for dead. Rob had watched them at it. Huge jaws that grabbed the trees by the trunk, one after another, ripped them out, dropped them, moved on. They could destroy an orchard in a day or two. When they were done it looked like a battlefield littered with corpses, row upon row of dead trees lying on their sides, their roots exposed. Later they came back with chippers the size of house trailers and ground the trees into piles of wood chips.

Peyton glanced at his watch.

Rob detoured back through the orchard, driving down a row of trees that nearly touched his SUV on either side, trees his grandfather had planted, some of them. There had been an old Philipino on the ranch when the boys were young, Pete Tima. He knew every tree in the orchard. He'd worked for Rob's grandfather, lived in a trailer out back of the orchard. Every day he'd walk through the orchard looking for blight, grafting new branches onto the old trees as a branch fell. Rob's father often checked in with Pete about insect infestations. He could feel blight conditions in his bones, he said. His rheumatism would kick up.

The first summer Rob was allowed to work in the orchard he was nine. He was charged with picking up "grounders," fallen pears that could be sold only for juice. He was paid ten cents a bucket. He had to keep a tally. As he dragged his bucket through the orchard, hot and hungry, he sometimes found at the end of a row a full bucket of "grounders" left for him by Pete.

When Rob was thirteen Pete insisted that he learn to graft, despite Rob's complete indifference to the idea. He wanted to learn to drive a fork lift. Rob could remember the humiliation of watching Pete peer through his Coke bottle eyeglasses and cut with the skill of a surgeon. Then Rob would try to follow his example with the dexterity and attention span of a six-foot, klutzy adolescent.

Some years ago Rob found Pete Tima asleep against a tree he had grafted a half dozen times over the years. He didn't wake up.

They passed a new block that Rob had planted himself, a red Bosc pear grafted onto dwarf rootstock that had thrived here. Pete Tima would have been proud of him.

He pulled up in front of the barn and turned off his engine. "You know, I oughta sell to you guys, but I'm not going to." His wife would kill him when he told her. She had her heart set on Paris. "I'll tough it out one more year."

"The price won't ever be this good," Peyton said.

"I know," Rob said.

"There's a lot of land available around here."

"I know," Rob said. Hell, every orchard in the Delta was for sale.

"It's a losing proposition. You know that."

"Yeah."

"Why don't you sleep on it," Peyton said. "We're in no hurry."

The young man fidgeted with his brief case again.

"I don't need to sleep on it," Rob said. "No deal." He headed into the barn, then turned.

"Be careful of those dogs," he said. He watched the men glance sideways over their shoulders.

"Those dogs are mean."

CPSIA information can be obtained at www.ICGtesting.com
Printed in the USA
LVOW12s0706300713

345221LV00001B/40/P

9 781475 994438